Strange Moon Press LLC
Presents


# HELP WANTED
# INQUIRE WITHIN

A Collection of Stories




ISBN 979-8-218-79920-5

Strange Moon Press LLC
10 Benning Street
Suite 160-168
West Lebanon, NH 03784
www.strangemoonpress.com

HELP WANTED
INQUIRE WITHIN

# V for Vern

by Cara M. Bassett

Vern stood with his suitcase and satchel held tightly to his bosom lest whatever growing on the uneven brick walls tried to reach out and take root. At his mother's behest he had hopped on a four-hour train ride to the metropolitan city, New Bayard, to care for his aging Great Aunt Marion. Vern had never met the woman but his mother spoke of her virtues endlessly. Her curiosity, her tenacity, her perseverance, her *wealth*.

Vern hadn't realized his mother's request would bring him *here,* though. To a narrow corridor with chipped tiled floors just begging for a lawsuit, and a single dingey light casting ghastly and flickering shadows across the door that he would have to knock on eventually. It wasn't even a bad building. He had been cautiously optimistic until a ride up three floors in a deathtrap of an elevator which turned him out into the glum hallway before him now.  He double- and triple-checked the neatly folded page of directions from his mother and wondered briefly if this was some kind of joke.

*Why did Aunt Marion live here?* According to his mother, the old woman had more than enough money to care for herself and yet chose to stay in the same building she'd lived in for decades. His mother had spent summers living here when she was Vern's age, although certainly it had been in better condition then.

He shouldered his satchel and took the final, brave steps to the door, pulling the sleeve of his shirt to cover his knuckle as he rapped three times. He was careful not to touch the frayed slip of paper tacked haphazardly between the door panels with rusted nails.

The sign read "Help Wanted: Inquire Within" and inquire he would. He would be doing quite a lot of *inquiring* over the phone this evening with his mother to find out why exactly she thought it was a good idea to send him on this ridiculous quest.

"Who is it?" came a sing-song voice; sweet but crisp, like an apple.

"Aunt Marion? It's Vernon Hern. Vidalia's son."

A series of hard knocking and sliding came from the other side of the door, making Vern flinch with each sound. Were those locks? Did Aunt Marion have… nine, ten, eleven locks? The poor woman was as afraid of the hideous building as Vern was. A wave of pity tugged at his heartstrings on her behalf.

The door opened just wide enough for a surprisingly strong arm to reach out and grab Vern by the collar, pulling him into the depths of a new world.

♦♦♦

Vern squinted in the dark room, trying to regain his senses. He heard each of the eleven locks re-bolt and then a *click* as a lamp was turned on, washing his strange surroundings in vibrant, blue light. Piles of books were stacked against the walls. Photos and note cards were pinned above them. Where some of the notecards ended, scribbled writing or drawings trailed onto the walls themselves.

There was a large opening across from the door which should have been a beautiful little breakfast nook but instead was taken up by a massive wooden desk burdened under loose papers and several decades worth of notebooks. Plastic bins labeled *Nov '91* and *Aug '02* were toppled sideways across the walkway, their contents spilling onto the floor: cassette tapes and newspaper clippings.

Jasmine incense was burning somewhere, a poor attempt to mask the mustiness. A cemetery of coffees lay at the base of the desk- single use and ceramic mugs alike were balanced on top of each other, almost impressively.

There was no way Vern's mother knew about all *this.*

"So, you're Vidalia's boy, eh?"

In his efforts to assess the bestrewn apartment, he had neglected to study the strange woman that had pulled him in. She was petite in stature but sturdy looking. A thick brown robe was pulled tightly around her round body, a collection of pendants and beaded necklaces peaked out from below the highly buttoned neckline.

A large pair of coke bottle glasses sat on her button nose, making her eyes appear much larger than they were. Her hair was mostly tucked under a pink satiny bonnet, but a few grey whisps had been pulled out in the commotion. The blue light masked any specific features that might have appeared beyond that.

Vern spotted a light switch by the door and leaned forward to flip it on. It washed the room in a harsh overhead light and set dust flying to the floor in waves as the blades of the fan began to spin.

Aunt Marion gave a gargled shriek and threw herself at the light switch, flipping the light off and plunging the room back into the blue glow.

"Are you insane?" She whispered hoarsely and then seemed to control herself, smoothing her robe and offering him a tight-lipped smile.

"At night, we use the blue light," she gestured to the hanging lantern, "or candlelight, but we *never ever, never* use the big light. Okay?"

She broke into a fit of coughing then, hacking into her sleeves and bending over so her other hand was on her knee. Vern grimaced and reached into his coat pocket to retrieve his handkerchief and offered it to her.

"Yes, yes," she said, waving the handkerchief away. "It's the damned dust, I'm fine."

She sucked in a breath and leaned back in a dramatic pose, as if taking a fuller look at the boy. Vern felt suddenly overdressed in his once-crisp buttoned shirt, mustard sweater vest, khaki dress pants and patent leather loafers. All of which were plastered to his body uncomfortably from the unseasonable heat.

Vern liked dressing nicer than his peers. *They*, who followed the whim of every fashion trend that graced the local mall. And he, infinitely classier in his timeless button downs and ironed pants. He was known to throw in a pair of well-fitting denim jeans with no holes or fraying from time to time. After all, even Wall Street had casual Fridays.

Vern dreamed of moving to a big city like this, albeit under different circumstances. He had the grades and passion to back those dreams up. He was already taking college-level classes and would graduate high school with half a degree under his belt. He'd even been offered a work study internship the following summer, which would put him in a good spot to graduate from high school with credits, experience, and style.

And yet all that seemed to disappear under the old woman's scrutiny. Her eyes settled on his sensible but stylish shoes and her face betrayed a slight grimace.

"Well, come on then," she croaked, the sweetness in her apple voice soured by the dust. She led him down a hidden hallway. "Let's take you to your room."

He plucked his suitcase from where it had fallen near the door and attempted to follow Aunt Marion through the maze of clutter.

Okay, so she was a hoarder. He had heard of people like that before. He didn't mind cleaning. They turned into a new room, and she flicked on another blue light lamp.

"Bathroom's next door. Only one, so don't hog it, okay? This is your room for the summer.  It ain't much, so let me know if you need anything specific."

The room was small, but clear of clutter, to Vern's delight. A daybed was pushed against one wall and the bedding was covered in a pattern of vines and some kind of berry, maybe blueberry? A quick sniff revealed the same pervasive dustiness but no signs of mold or decay. A simple wooden chest sat at the foot of the bed and a folding dinner tray table had been set up by the window on the opposite wall. In the middle of the dinner tray sat a soda bottle with a pinch of flowers in its mouth.

Vern was warmed by the gesture and turned to thank her for the flowers, but Aunt Marion was gone, having presumably returned to bed for the night.

He set his suitcase on the wooden chest and lowered himself onto the bedspread, taking stock of every creak of the old springs. He pulled out his cellphone and checked for service.  One timid bar blinked in and out. Vern sighed and placed the phone back into its pocket.

With the curveballs he'd been thrown that evening, staying positive felt like quite a challenge, but he was determined to try. Facing adversity with a positive attitude was just the kind of thing top recruiters looked for in applicants. Plus, this summer was bound to make one hell of an admissions essay.

♦♦♦

Vern woke at 5:30 a.m. on the dot, as he had every day for the past three years. He had just enough time to remember where he was and stretch when a light creak sounded by the door. A large pair of eyes peered in at him, seemingly surprised to find him staring back.

"Oh good, you're awake." Aunt Marion said, opening the door and crossing to the window draped in black-out curtains. The sweetness had returned to her voice from the night before, however without the crispness he had originally imagined. It was richer, brighter. Less of an apple and more of a plum.

She flung the curtains back just as the first rays of dawn filtered in, outlining the shadow of the apartment building next door.

"Sun's up, we're up. That's a rule here, so it's a good thing you're an early riser like me. Breakfast is in the kitchen." She exited the room and closed the door thoughtfully behind her.

Vern dressed in denim jeans with no holes or frays, for even though it wasn't Friday, the apartment seemed to call for a more casual dress code. He slipped on an undershirt and a short-sleeved button up, having learned his lesson about the heat yesterday. He slipped on his patent leather loafers and exited the small room, taking a deep breath beforehand as though preparing to dive into water.

The "breakfast in the kitchen" turned out to be fresh coffee from a pot coated in a thick patina. There was an open box of bran cereal on top of the fridge next to an unopened box of Fruity-O's.

Vern grabbed the box of bran and found a bowl in one of the cupboards, which he rinsed out in the sink. He opened a fridge covered in magnetic notepads and was relieved that the smell of decay was not coming from it. He was, however, disappointed to see a lack of milk and dumped the cereal back into the box, then returned the bowl to the cupboard in defeat.

Aunt Marion swept into the room, no longer in her brown robe. Instead, she wore a light blue jumpsuit and a thick pocketed belt that made her look like a me-

4

chanic. She poured herself a bowl of bran and dumped coffee into it and began to crush the cereal with her spoon as she read a daily newspaper from 1997.

The morning light that filtered through the various windows drew many features to light that Vern had been unable to see in the blue tint of the lamp the night before. Deep-set lines accented her rouged cheeks and her hair was done up into an array of tight grey and black curls. The necklaces she'd been wearing under her robe last night had not moved. Many were beaded, some were simple cords, some carried heavy pendants that stacked on top of each other. They looked to be woven or knotted into each other and Vern wondered if she ever took them off or if they were a permanent feature of her slightly humped neck.

She was old but decidedly not as frail as his mother had said. She was in her mid-eighties, give or take a decade. But seeing the state of her apartment in the morning light was proof enough to Vern that the woman was in desperate need of his help.

"So," Vern wagered, seeking a personable question with which to start the conversation, "What are your plans for the day?"

Marion took a moment to finish the sentence she was reading, tracing the words with a long, blue nail. Eventually, the paper dropped to the table and she studied him over the wide edge of her glasses.

"Your mother assured me that you were self-sufficient and could entertain yourself. I'm a very busy woman and I don't have time to share plans or babysit. Here," she slid a key and a hundred-dollar bill across the table at him and lifted her paper again. He lifted the items while she took a bite of her coffee-and-bran. "The door is not to be opened unless you are coming or going. That key will let you in during the day, but if you're not inside by nine PM, you will be locked out via the security locks. The money is for you to have fun, enjoy the city, et cetera, et cetera. If you need any groceries or toiletries, leave a note on the fridge. Now, if you'll excuse me, I have much to do."

With that, she set the newspaper on the table and scurried to the door. She draped a thin brown vest over her shoulders, grabbed an umbrella, and slipped out the door without another word.

Vern took a deep breath and slipped back into the kitchen to clean the remnants of her breakfast. He washed the mountain of dishes in the sink and scrubbed the bottom of the coffee pot meticulously. When he found the source of the mold smell, an unfinished frozen dinner at the bottom of the sink, he proudly disposed of it properly (And, thanks to the gloves and face masks he packed for just such occasions, with minimal gagging).

When that was done, he did a quick tidying of the rest of the room. He swept, straightened the rug, and realigned the books and newspapers on the small kitchen table. Satisfied with his progress and reminded by his stomach of his mortal need for breakfast, he snatched the key, money and a few things from his bag, then left the strange apartment to explore New Bayard.

♦♦♦

When Vern finally found a nearby cafe, he ordered a steamed milk tea and blueberry muffin and then tried to call his mother. She, of course, did not answer. She was at work. A single text from the night before shone on his LED screen:

*Give Auntie Marion all my love. XOXO -M*

He took a sip of the still-cooling tea and drafted a return text, unsure how much to say about his strange situation.

*Got in safe. Call me when you can. Love you. -S*

He counted his remaining cash, $86.07, and set to searching for things to do for the day on his phone. There was a Museum of Science and Anatomy within walkable distance that boasted a special discount for students during the weekday and thus his morning plans were set into motion. He took to the sidewalk with his overpriced tea and mediocre muffin, feeling like a true metropolitan man.

A flock of grey and white pigeons flew overhead, making Vern duck and cover. He narrowly dodged a gob of poop that landed to his left. The flock landed in a pavilion to the right of him, where a girl with rainbow-colored hair and a matching crocheted top was leaning against a waist-high brick wall, feeding them with seed out of a burlap bag. Vern considered calling out to her to control her animals but decided to count his losses and persevere forward.

He crossed the street to avoid a block of outdoor vendors that shouted dollar amounts and brand names, promising their legitimacy at a price you couldn't say no to. An argument in another language broke out amongst two patrons and Vern swallowed tightly as he raced along the sidewalk.

*What had his mother gotten him into?*

His mother couldn't have known about the state of Aunt Marion—or the entire city, for that matter—when she sent him out here. She surely would never have gone through with it had she known how bad things were.

Still, he had made a promise to his mother to care for Aunt Marion over the course of the summer. And now, having seen the state of things at her apartment, Vern knew how deeply and truly he was needed here. It felt sort of good to know how desperately you were needed somewhere. Vern smiled to himself and held his nose as he gave an alley with a literal dumpster fire a wide berth.

♦♦♦

The museum was interesting enough and, mercifully, air conditioned. A few of the displays appeared to be slightly misinformed or out of date, but he decided to write a thorough review explaining the necessary updates.

A wide balcony of second floor displays circled a herd of replica mammoth skeletons. It seemed that most people walked around the display and returned down the stairs, seldom venturing into the little dimly lit display room in the far corner. Noticing this, Vern wound his way up the circling staircases and meandered through the trickling crowd of snickering youths and parents pushing baby strollers.

The sign above the entrance read in tight letters, <u>Cryptozoological Biology: The Evidence of Cryptids in New Bayard</u>.

Determined to see every inch of the museum to allow the most cohesive feedback he could provide (and extend his time in the air conditioning), he entered the small room. Inside were fossils and bones with descriptions of the breakoff of genus families millions of years ago.

Old journals were propped open to pages detailing encounters with creatures of strange and unusual abilities. Some could fly or had healing properties, others could conjure thoughts of your greatest fears. Drawings and blurry photos of forests with circles around dark blotches that were reportedly "not what they seemed."

The display claimed these creatures to be both great and small, both docile and violent, both dumb and smart. So smart, in fact, that they could at times rival the intelligence of humans. Was it likely that there were giant human-like creatures living in suburban or urban settings and completely unrecognized by modern science? No. Of course not. But according to this funny little science project in the back of an otherwise moderately reasonable museum, it was more likely than one might think.

Vern was phrasing his review of the egregiously preposterous display to the museum's director when he spotted the plaque near the entrance of the small alcove, nearly covered by one of the glass cases carrying a wide array of knives and bullets claimed to have maimed or injured real cryptids.

The plaque read: *This display has been generously funded and sourced by friend of the museum, Dr. Marion J Hern.*

♦♦♦

Vern spent the afternoon cleaning the entryway, dusting away cobwebs and sweeping debris from the room. He cleaned the hallway to the apartment as well, leaving the front door open and letting the sunlight into the dim space as he did so. He went searching for a replacement light for the hallway and found the box of blue bulbs in a kitchen cupboard. It wasn't ideal but if it didn't flicker, it was a step in the right direction.

He wet a few rags with warm water and dish soap and scrubbed at the walls, determined to clean the best he could while he was there, and thinking about how to tell his mother about what he'd found.

When the light began to dim, he re-entered the apartment and pulled a chair from the kitchen in to wipe the dusty blades of the fan.

Vern cooked himself a delicious dinner of pork chops, couscous, and a fresh lemon vinaigrette salad, the ingredients of which he picked up on his way back home from the museum along with a carton of milk, a bag of pretzels, and a few honey-crisp apples.

He found himself feeling an anticipatory nostalgia for the summer he could've had. He could have cooked good, healthy meals for himself and his poor, sickly aunt every day. Kept her fed and entertained reading Melville and Austen. Maybe she would have left the apartment to him in her will and he could have moved in after high school and put a framed photo of the two of them on the wall above his sensible couch, in memoriam for the summer he spent with his darling, wealthy, great aunt.

After a long day of walking, cleaning, and lamenting how things should have gone, he allowed himself the luxury of a long, hot shower.

He hadn't known that she was a doctor of anything, let alone zoology or cryptozoology or whatever it was she had studied.

As he cleaned the house, he realized many of the books pertained to cryptozoology. There were titles such as *Cryptids & You: A Study on the Effect of Cryptozoology on Psychology, Help! There's a Bigfoot in My Backyard!, Alternate Biology: In Defense of Cryptozoology,* and *The Complete History of Cryptids: Volume IV.*

Some of the newspaper clippings talked of strange, sick, or unidentifiable creatures, run-ins or local attacks. Personal ads for missing pets, missing children, or advertising meetups of support groups for unspecified "survivors." The cassette tapes weren't labeled beyond their dates, but he had no doubt they had something to do with cryptids as well.

She was certainly passionate about the topic.

He tried to call his mother twice, but his service was still dismally poor and even his texts were returning as undeliverable. He was tired from his efforts and decided to try again tomorrow. Although he had been set on helping Aunt Marion, surely his mother would want to bring him right back home after learning what the old woman was mixing herself up with.

He was dressed in a comfy, red satin pajama set and reading by the light of the blue lamp in his room when he heard the front door lock being unlatched. Once she was inside, Aunt Marion quickly set to locking all eleven of the inside locks. He listened as she fumbled around in the entryway. He waited for her to say something about his cleaning efforts or mention the food in the kitchen, but her tired footsteps waddled quietly up the hall and past his room without a word. Her bedroom door swung shut and that was that.

♦♦♦

The boy woke to the warbling grunt of a struggle or skirmish that had broken out somewhere in the apartment. He heard a series of thumps as a stack of books was knocked over. A cry was cut short by a loud snapping noise and a few angry curses in Aunt Marion's plummy voice.

Vern jumped out of bed and slipped on his patent leather loafers, but before he could reach the door, it swung open. Aunt Marion flipped the lamp on and stood holding a thin-barreled pistol in her right hand. Her eyes dashed around the room frantically and his stomach tied itself in knots.

She shoved past him to the wooden chest, knocking over his open suitcase, which sent his belongings sprawling across the floor. She held the gun to the open chest as if expecting something to be waiting for her on the other side. When she didn't find anything, she started rifling through the bedding, her collar of tangled necklaces crashing against each other cacophonously. She didn't leave a single layer of the bed unturned and stripped the bed down to the mattress before flinging it to the ground, her strength impressing and terrifying Vern.

Determining the bed to be sufficiently searched, she turned to the window and reached for the curtain.

"What is going on?" Vern sobbed. He was scared to the bone and wanted nothing more than to call his mother and be rid of this strange, crazed woman. She spun around, holding the gun high in the air. The blue light gave her a ghostly appearance and Vern thought his heart might jump through his chest.

"You left the door open. Don't deny it. I watched the building's security tapes and I saw the whole thing. While you were busy *cleaning* and disobeying my very simple instructions, you let not one but *two* harpies in. *Harpies!*"

This crazed woman was going to shoot him and his bones would wind up in a glass case at the Museum of Biology and Anatomy with a plaque labeled "frog person" or "moth man."

He was never going to see his mother again.

She turned back to the curtain and flung it aside, streetlight flooding in and the glass bottle of flowers crashed to the floor. A fluttering figure began to desperately bang at the window. He couldn't make out the details of its backlit shape, but it looked to be approximately the size of a chicken.

Aunt Marion took a large step back, aimed the gun, and without hesitation, fired.

A small cloud of smoke filled the room and the bird fell to the floor in a heavy heap. The shot wasn't nearly as loud as Vern was led to believe guns were, not that he had a drop of experience with the matter. He didn't see any blood and could hardly see anything at all in the infuriating blue light, but he began to feel lightheaded and nauseous.

Aunt Marion pushed past him and he slid down the wall onto the floor, hanging his head between his knees and trying to calm his raging heartbeat.

Okay, so maybe the old woman wasn't so crazy after all. Confused, sure, but there *had* been an animal in his room. A fat pigeon of some kind or somebody's pet chicken that had gotten loose; he wasn't sure exactly. He didn't want to get close enough to find out.

When Aunt Marion returned, she was dragging a black duffel bag. She walked to the window and carefully picked up the creature by its feet, struggling to lift it into the bag and getting to her knees to fit it all the way in. Once finished, she zippered the bag shut and looked up at Vern accusatorially.

"Are you going to throw up?"

"I don't know," Vern admitted.

"Are you going to faint?"

Vern shook his head miserably. "I don't think so."

"Well, come on. We've got to get these things to Doc. They won't stay down forever."

"You mean they're *alive?*" He asked incredulously.

They both rose unsteadily to their feet.

"Those were wax bullets infused with rhubarb. It'll keep them down for a while but not forever. Come on."

She walked to the door and pushed past him for the third time of the night. He followed her and she paused, turning to him.

"Are you going to get the bag or not?" she asked.

He swallowed hard and went back into his trashed room and gingerly lifted the straps. He gagged at the feel of their body weight adjusting limply in the bag.

Back in the entryway, Aunt Marion facing the covered window behind her desk.

"We'll be there in fifteen," she clamped the receiver of an old landline and slammed a drawer of her desk closed. She strapped the pistol to her hip and grabbed the thin brown vest she'd put on before she left last time.

"I need to change, get my—" he began.

She silenced him with a single, wrinkled finger. "No time. We need to go *now.*"

♦♦♦

"The Doc" turned out to be a veterinarian at a twenty-four hour emergency clinic around two blocks from Aunt Marion's apartment building.

Vern dutifully carried the heavy bag the entire way in the elevator and down the two streets. He lamented the sweat stains he'd have to carefully clean out of his satin clothes with vinegar when they returned. As they entered the street-level clinic, a bell echoed against the white tile floor, announcing their arrival.

Doc entered the room in a pair of slacks, navy blue collared shirt, and a white lab coat that reflected the bright fluorescent lights. The sight of someone dressed in business casual lab attire put Vern at ease. *Finally, a professional.*

"I'm Dr. Lesley. You must be Vern. Your aunt has told me all about you." Her clipped speech almost made Vern question what he was hearing. Aunt Marion told her about Vern? When? What had she said?

Dr. Lesley nodded to the bag on Vern's shoulder. "Are these them?" She looked to be in her forties, with a stethoscope and pair of reading glasses hanging delicately around her slim neck.

"Yes, these are the," Aunt Marion looked around the empty room as if checking for eavesdroppers and then whispered "*harpies.*"

Vern cringed in embarrassment at his aunt's delusions but kept a brave face for the doctor's sake.

"Where should I put them?" He asked, his shoulders aching under the pressing weight.

"Come this way," Dr. Lesley said curtly. Her lab coat billowed out as she briskly led Marion and Vern to a surgical room in the back of the clinic that smelled of sharp cleaning agents and iron.

He lifted the bag onto one of the surgery tables at the doctor's behest and excused himself as they started to unzip the bag, not wanting to see whatever bloody mess laid inside.

Dr. Lesley gave Vern a sympathetic smile. "My daughter is in the other room if you'd like to find her. She can help you find the snacks."

Even though Vern wasn't particularly interested in snacks right then, the thought of finding the doctor's daughter sounded like a fine idea. In that moment he wanted nothing more than to surround himself with *sane, normal* people.

Passing white walls decorated with a smattering of animal-themed motivational posters, Vern glanced into each room until he found one full of boarding kennels. There was one lone resident, a medium-sized skin and bones terrier, pale brown and grey-muzzled with eyes glossed over and more than one snaggletooth. It stood hunched over in the crate, not from lack of space, but simply from lack of ability to straighten.

From behind the row of stainless-steel cages came a young girl roughly Vern's age, wearing a tie-dye shirt that read "3rd Str Vet Clinic." The bright colors on the shirt matched the girl's brightly colored hair.

"I know you," Vern surprised himself by saying.

The girl looked up, confused.

"You're the girl with the pigeons."

She rolled her eyes as though accustomed to that title and returned her attention to the kennels. Her rainbow hair was pulled back into a single, thick braid. She stood with one hand raised halfway to the kennel door, holding a meaty treat for which the elderly dog was already salivating. It was the girl he had seen on the street that morning, feeding the flock of pigeons.

The girl shifted uncomfortably and glanced around, "Did you come in with the doc?"

It was Vern's turn to be confused. "No, Aunt Marion and I came to see the doc—" The old dog barked, then, or what Vern could assume was the remnants of a bark. It was more of a breathy screech, but it communicated its impatience well enough and the girl put the treat between the kennel bars. It gobbled the thing whole, not bothering to use its few remaining teeth.

"Dr. Hern is your aunt then?" She said, wiping grease from the treat off on her cargo shorts.

"Oh, I—" Vern stuttered, remembering the plaque at the museum that honored his crazy aunt as a *doctor.* "I suppose she is. I thought you meant Dr. Lesley—"

"She's my mom. Why would I call her *doc*?"

Vern didn't know what to say to that and so he opted not to respond at all and looked at the dog, which was turning in circles in its cage.

"What's the matter with it?"

"Lady's just old. Nothing's wrong with her." The girl said forcefully and Vern wagered he had breached a sensitive subject. The dog plopped onto the dog bed in the kennel and sighed.

"Listen, I think we got off on the wrong foot. My name is Vern," he said, holding out his hand.

"Like the plant?" She asked, accepting the hand cautiously.

"No, *Vern* with a V, short for Vernon."

"Oh. Well, I'm Abbi."

"It's a pleasure to meet you." Abbi smiled a little but dropped Vern's hand.

"Mutual, I'm sure," she said in an accent and Vern couldn't decide yet if he was being made fun of.

"So… Do you work here?" Vern asked.

"Not typically, but since it's summer, Mom said I could hang out with Lady whenever she works nights. I'd probably be up anyway and this way she can *make sure I don't get into any trouble.*" She said in a deep voice that was a rough approximation of her mother's warm timbre. Abbi shrugged, smiling again, "I don't mind, though. I like keeping Lady company," she glanced at the old dog lovingly and stuck a finger in the kennel, which Lady didn't notice through her heavy snores.

Vern was debating whether to ask about Lady, as the girl so clearly liked to talk about her, or the girl's age, which Vern was excessively curious about. Before he could decide, he noticed her looking at him sideways and grew self-conscious.

"Are you really the doc's nephew? Like, by blood? You don't look much like her."

"I really am. On my dad's side, at least. And… I've been told I take after my mom, so that might be why…"

"She's really cool," Abbi admitted, leaning against Lady's kennel. "She's one of the most badass old broads I've ever met. Like, *really.*"

He could see the resemblance between Abbi and her mother in the eyes and shape of the chin, and the tone of her voice. Aside from her eccentric hair, she seemed to be a relatively reasonable person and decided he'd have to trust her. He looked out into the hall and then back at her, taking a solemn step forward.

"I don't know how well you know her," he began delicately. "But I think she might need serious help."

Abbi's eyes widened, and Vern, validated and grateful, continued.

"Her house is a mess. A hoarder situation, really. She has books and old tapes and things all over the walls. And she seems to really believe in…" His voice grew so quiet on the next word it was more of a mouth than a whisper, "*cryptids.* You know, like, Bigfoot and chupacabra and whatnot. She thinks those things we brought in tonight are harpies. I think she might be in deep stage psychosis or dementia or something."

Abbi's wide eyes conveyed a multitude of emotions, none of which Vern was capable of understanding. Her mouth opened and her head tilted, as if trying to think of the right words to say and Vern grew concerned that he had said too much.

"I'm serious, just ask her, she has all these *locks* and a wax gun and pictures and a chalkboard and-"

Abbi held up her finger, shushing him. He shushed.

"Did you see those things you brought in tonight? The… harpies?"
"Not really."
"I think you should follow me."

♦♦♦

Abbi walked through the hallway, her flat sneakers squelching with every step as though she recently walked through something wet.

The rainbow-headed girl led Vern back to the surgery room. Vern paused, not wanting to see what carnage lay beyond but Abbi put her hand gently on Vern's back and urged him forward.

"Just, *look*," she said.

Vern took a deep breath and peeked into the room.

Dr. Lesley stood over the table, a light fixture angled down to illuminate the feathered creature below. Aunt Marion sat on a stool between the table and the door but turned upon hearing them enter.

"Hey, Doc," Abbi said. Aunt Marion stood and opened her arms wide, smiling at the young girl and hobbling towards her for a hug. They exchanged pleasantries and Aunt Marion remarked on how tall she was getting, her long blue nails glinting as she pinched the girl's cheeks.

But Vern wasn't paying attention to that. His stomach flipped and his knees threatened to buckle. He stared at the head of a woman, covered with long hair-like feathers, lying unconscious on Dr. Lesley's table. Where the head transitioned to neck, brown, white and black feathers burst into a rotund, plump body. Wings lay expanded across the table, balancing carelessly off the edge as the veterinarian worked to stitch the broken skin. He could see the chest rising and falling with the assistance of medical wires and a tube down its angular mouth.

It was a creature like Vern had never seen before. A monster, a harpy… *a cryptid.*

Vern then, finally, fainted.

♦♦♦

When he woke, Vern was face to face with glowing white eyes and jagged teeth. Like a monster from his nightmares come to life, the creature opened its mouth and the smell of death unfurled.

He was thrashing and screaming when Abbi came running into the room, pulling the beast far enough back for Vern to catch his breath. "Relax, it's just Lady."

As the horrible face was pulled back, Vern recognized it as belonging to the old dog, and not a monster at all. The strangeness of the night came pounding back into his head.

Whatever excuse he came up with—a trick of the light, a magical hoax, hallucinogenic poisoning, sudden-onset schizophrenia—nothing struck him quite like the truth.

Monsters were real.

Cryptids were real.

*Aunt Marion was right.*

"You okay?" Abbi asked once Vern's breathing had slowed. He blinked one eye open and then, unwillingly, the other.

He was lying in the boarding room, a towel rolled up under his head with a raggedy blanket that smelled of detergent thrown over top. A wet washcloth lay in a lump beside him as though it had at one time been draped across his forehead.

As he sat up a throbbing pain ricocheted through his temple. He wiped crusted drool from the corner of his mouth and smoothed his ruffled hair. He felt as though the ground had been ripped beneath his feet, literally.

"What happened?" Vern croaked.

"You fell pretty hard. Stayed asleep for like four hours? It's almost time for the day shift to start. Doc went home like an hour ago, said to let you sleep. But I was just on my way to wake you," Abbi helped to lift him from the cold, tiled floor.

"Does your head hurt? Mom said you could take this to help with the pain." She lifted a bottle of unmarked white pills from her pocket which Vern declined warily. "Well, Dr. Chance will be here before too long, so, it's probably best if you head back home now."

Vern dazedly shuffled to the front door. Lady screeched a goodbye to him as he went.

"Do you need me to walk you home?"

As his eyes adjusted to the rising sun, Vern found that he could see the apartment building from where they stood. Being able to walk himself home in his red satin pajamas was one of the few dignities he had left.

"I've got it." He said, beginning his limp onward.

"Y'know, I wasn't kidding when I said Doc Marion is cool." Vern paused, turning back to look at Abbi. "She's really smart and stuff. Maybe you can see that, now… now that you know she isn't crazy, and all. I'll see you around, Vern."

♦♦♦

Vern stood in the dark hallway in his sweat-stained satin pajamas and scuffed patent leather loafers. The narrow corridor's chipped tiled floors were freshly scrubbed, and the single exposed bulb cast a steady and bright blue glow across the door. The sign reading *Help Wanted: Inquire Within* in his great aunt's sprawling script stared back at him.

The door, to his surprise, was unlocked and he stepped inside delicately, quickly closing it behind him. The curtains were flung open, light filtering onto the piles of books and records. He ran a finger along one of the books, wondering how much of the contents were true. How much knowledge had he swept aside as non-sense before last night?

The box marked *Aug '02* was on the floor again. A dusty old brown vest that matched his aunt's stuffed in the side. A photo album had been pulled to the top and flipped to reveal a picture of Aunt Marion, looking twenty years younger. Beside her stood a dark smudge of a creature with only two white spots where eyes would be. Next to it stood something that looked like a large naked mole rat. It was covered in wrinkles and the size of a hog, water seemed to seep from its eyes and formed dark stains at its feet, but it offered a warty smile for the camera. And on the other side of it, with one hand scratching the beast's ear affectionately, stood a very young but indisputable image of Vern's mother.

"She apprenticed with me for three summers, you know. That's how she met my nephew, your father."

Vern turned to see Aunt Marion standing by the door with her arms folded. Her necklaces jingled as she shook her head wistfully.

Vern looked back to the album and flipped through the pages, seeing image after image of irrefutable proof that cryptids were real.

"I don't get it. Why not tell everyone they're real? If you have proof, why display blurry images and journals at the Museum?"

Aunt Marion sighed and rested against a stack of books. "I'm not a *monster hunter*. I don't do this for glory. I'm a researcher, a conservationist. I teach people to *believe* because that's the best I can do without putting the cryptids in danger.

"Since I was your age, it has been my life's mission to protect them as best as I can. There are dangerous people in the world who would capture or kill these creatures if it meant a chance at the magic they possess. For the animal's sakes and ours, I keep them at bay."

The silence sat between them as Vern lifted the brown vest from the box. It was wrinkled and musty, but the embroidered "V" on the left shoulder stood out in blue thread.

"You can return home, if you'd like." Aunt Marion said, looking away from him. "There's a train leaving in three hours. You don't have to help like your mother arranged. But now that you know the truth, you will have to swear to keep their secret. Just like your mother *and* father did. Like Doc and Abbi have. And many others before you."

He stood there, frazzled, exhausted, and amazed at the world she'd opened to him.

His mother knew about this all along.

*V for Vidalia.*

She sent him here on purpose so he would learn the truth and help. And help, he would.

*V for Vern.*

Vern raised his hand honorifically, "I swear it. And, I'd like to stay, if that's all right. I have *so much* to learn."

Aunt Marion mulled his seriousness over and then nodded to herself and disappeared suddenly into the hallway. For a moment, Vern wondered if she'd left for the day and felt robbed of the dramatic embrace he'd felt certain was coming. Then, he heard a ripping sound and the door re-opened.

Aunt Marion tightly rolled the aged sign from her front door, each of the four corners jagged where she'd torn it down. There was a note of emotion in her voice, deep and rich, less like a plum than a sweet potato.

"Well, no rest for the weary. Get yourself cleaned up. And put on that vest. *We* have much to do." She said, a note of emotion clenching at her throat.

It wasn't an embrace, but the gesture was dramatic enough to satisfy Vern.

He carried the thin, brown vest—worn first by his mother and now to be worn by him—into the depths of the apartment to prepare for his first day as an apprentice cryptozoologist.

# The Light Follower

## by Ivan Davis

*Lights: my slumbers are filled to the brim with visions of the lights of heaven. Blue lights, red lights, big lights, small lights, dancing in a cosmic festival.*

*I chase them, they give me a tidal wave of hope for a brighter day.*

*I hope for a resolution to my pain, an end to my restless nights, yet they lead me in a circle, a wheel of forever torment in which I may not escape.*

*I pursue, in ever growing quickness, yet like Apollo I cannot overtake.*

*I strive and strive, till I cannot strive anymore.*

### Chapter I: Les Misérables of America

"Wake up, wake up, Father! Father, wake up!" My little Susanne shouted, tugging upon my collared shirt.

"Eh, Susanne… why do you disturb my slumber?" I replied, half-heeding, as sunlight beamed into my eyes and I slowly crept back under my bed sheets.

"Father, may I join the other kids outside in a game?" Susanne replies, scrunching her little face in a way that she knows I cannot deny.

"Fine, but make sure you are back home by three o'clock. Mrs. Morgan next door said she is going to make an apple pie for all the children on the street."

She jumps off my hungry tummy, screaming in excitement all the way down the dirt street on which our shack sits.

I sat a few more moments in my bed, planning out the day that awaited me, another day unemployed, in need of an economic savior.

I grabbed my patched-up coat and dusty hat, already the cold winds of the Hudson River whistled through the walls of my half-baked shack. I opened my door, with a frozen front slapping my face back and forth as I entered the world.

Skidding down to the soup line, set up by the kind and humble St. Marks Church to ensure good fellas like me can see another day. I pounced to get in line, hoping to catch some soup before the pots dry up. I earwigged into the two fellows in front of me discussing the few jobs all of us are chasing.

"I heard there was help wanted sign for *two* jobs on Chambers Street, I guess those policies Roosevelt was putting out are working after all."

"Why are we waiting here in line then, my stomach can wait, but my pockets can't!"

"Calm down, there ain't no shot I was getting a job at a library, I'm missing ten of my teeth! And you ain't in a better situation yourself, you need all your fingers to open a book."

I looked up instantaneously; my frown instantly turns upside down as that very library had been my dwelling prior to the markets crashing. I quickly jumped out of line, rushing towards the exit of this maze of slums built up among the East Village.

I remember exactly where the library is, two blocks south and three blocks east of Robinsons Café, where my once lavish apartment with electricity sat above prior to this great depression of our times knocked me off my high horse. I knew my prayers had been answered and that I had finally caught that light in my dreams.

Bright days were ahead for me and Susanne!

I made it onto Broadway, already envisioning the bright future ahead of me. I stopped to catch a breath, glancing upon the massive structures of splendid design around me.

These monuments give me passion; I saw them as a metaphor for me rising above the filthy streets below to the clear skies above. I continued forth, like Odysseus in the Odyssey, one of my favorites to pick up from the mass of books in the library I will once more wander through. I made it on to Chambers Street, but my heart sinks to my feet the moment I turned my eyes upon the Municipal Library and see a mass of desperate men wanting to squeeze their tiny percentage of a chance at a life worth living.

I leapt into the crowd, cooking up a plan to escape the hoard before it consumed my only hope of light is ceased before my eyes.
I was sweating like an iced beer on a summer's day. My heart pounded like a swing from James J. Braddock straight to the face.

My guarantee at a life beyond this nightmare seems more like an illusion, a facade that has dragged me along. I waited for an hour or two in the ever-growing crowd, which seemed to double as time dragged on while the line seemed to remain ever stagnant.

I stared at the exquisite library reminiscing of the days as a young man. I visited that great sanctuary of books nearly every day in my youth. While the other boys were out hopping the hopscotch tiles, I was hopping from book to book, intrenching myself in the world of words I found comfort in. As I grew in height so did my life grow outside those walls, and I slowly drifted away.

I had to provide for my family, working job to job until luck bumped into me, literally, as me and the old librarian Mr. Earlston nearly walked straight into each other. He instantly recognized me as the little boy who would ask him to fetch a book from the top shelf and struck up an hour-long conversation between the two of us. He was going to be retiring, having played the stock market with his decent wages, he had acquired an estate on the Hudson north of here. He offered me a job at the library, and without hesitation I accepted his offer.

I woke from my daydreaming as a larger fella in front of me was distracted in a conversation with another unfortunate son. I sneakily skipped ahead of him, but not a second passed before his strong fist grabs my coat and tossed me backwards "What the hell are you doing, chub!"

"I'm sorry, I didn't know you were in the line." I replied, hoping to avoid a knuckle sandwich.

"Stay in your place, or I'll have to keep you there!" The pig- faced man furiously shouted as he encroached, his spit soaking my face. He continued to confront me, shouting goblin-like words I could barely comprehend.

The mass of stress on my shoulders collapsed, and I felt nearly possessed, unable to control my fist as it flew straight into his disgusting face. Pigface backhanded me in an instant.

I swung around like a tornado down to the hard, dirty ground.

After that moment, darkness.

"Are you all right, sir!" The officer said, staring down at me like a caring adult looks down on a child.

"I'm fine." I replied quietly, trying to right my brittle self. "Can you tell me what happened?" He guides me to a nearby bench. I looked up to the once crowded entrance, now nearly barren with only a hand full of fellows standing around.

I quickly made up a story that will ensure I won't spend the night in jail. "I was in line and then this man accused me of cutting ahead, I confronted him, and he then attacked me like a savage dog. I tried holding my own, but he had the advantage and must have knocked me out." I replied.

"The other fella said you were cutting in line, but I don't have any witnesses that noticed. I would suggest you just head hospital to get that black eye taken care of."

I gingerly touched my pounding face. "But what of the library job, I once worked there and know I had a chance!" I shouted in a state of hopeless frustration.

"I'm sorry sir, but the library said they hired two fellas early in the morning, but they got intimidated by the crowd when they tried taking the sign down." He patted me on the back and pulled me to my feet and back into the world.

I was at a dead end in life. Despair threatened to tear me apart. I walked down Broadway, filled with people who had been given a chance at a life worth living; driving fancy vehicles, dressed like kings, and eating like such. I glanced once more at the monuments of the sky around, wishing to arise like they have, away from the drama and conflict of the ground I rely on. My eyes traveled back to Earth, and I continued my journey home.

I passed a pharmacy on Walter Street, and at that moment tears began to fall from my eyes, thinking of my little Susanne. When we conceived her, I had such hopes of a bright future for us, but once she came on to this world my luck seemingly ceased. My lovely wife had passed upon her birth, then the market crashed in '29 and I lost everything I had worked so hard to gain.

At that moment the hair on my neck stood up and a shrieking buzz echoed into my right ear. I turned my head to see a hidden alley and my eyes fell upon a door bearing a sign of hope, a sign signifying that help was wanted!

I was in pure shock and I felt as though I was still in a state of delirium. I escorted my bruised and battered self into the alley, limping past piles of uncollected trash, scurrying rats snatching up remains of rotten meals of a bygone hour. I approached the door, feeling an intense sensation of weariness as I stared at the crooked panels, the lettering on the sign as red as blood.

I presumed it to be some sort of butcher shop, or perhaps even a secret booze operation, taking advantage of the ever-growing black market. Wherever this trail might lead me, I have no more options. The life of myself and my daughter depends on this route.

I opened the door, peeking into a stairway that led down to a wooden cellar door with lights beaming from beneath its frame, and a large golden clock hanging on a piercing metal pole in the wall.

Intrigued, I walked down the stairs, already rehearsing the masterclass of words I shall present to the owner of this establishment.

As I placed my feet in front of the entrance, I stared into the golden clock, it's little but ever interesting designs give visions of Big Ben in London as I have imagined it from my time in the tales of Sherlock Homes. The steady ticking enshrines the passing of time, an idea that is slowly slipping out of my old man hands. I took two deep breaths and took my first steps into a new life ahead.

### Chapter II: 20,000 Leagues Under New York

I found myself in a small diner, not so elegant as the other fine establishments on Broadway or on 3$^{rd}$ Ave, and it seemed to be one of the speakeasies I heard about in the paper, set up by gangsters like Lucky Luciano to funnel boot-legged beverages into the city. It was relatively empty, only two fellows huddled at a corner table and a bartender cleaning up his station. I walked up to the bar counter, and with a deep breath, I began a conversation.

"Hello." I said awkwardly as the bar tender turns slowly towards me, anchoring a large grin covered under a thick long black mustache.

"Hello there, how may I help you today?" He replied in a thick Italian accent as though he just got off the boat from Sicily.

"I'm looking for work and I stumbled upon your establishment. I'm good at about everything and if there's anything I'm not good at I'll be damned."

He responded quickly. "Sorry, mister, but I got that job filled up this morning, I forgot to fetch that sign down. Sorry." He refused to look me in the eye and face the demons slowly pulling themselves out of my eye sockets. He silently turned back to his work at the bar.

I stood there, completely motionless, burning up my last dose of free will to ensure I neither fall into a forever unconscious state nor strangling the Italian bastard to death. I took a final breath, pushing my entire structure high above my slouched position, and into a being of higher power. I gripped my fist as hard as I could, staring intensely into the man's soul, even with his face opposing mine.

"Sir." I replied with a tidal wave of confidence flowing throughout the room. "Yes, my good sir. I am at the end of my road, seemingly the end of my story that I believed would go on till I was old and decrypted, not at the age of 27. I had a future forged ahead, me and my daughter, we were to live a splendid life on my once great compensation, but now I have but a nickel in my pocket. I'm going to walk these roads until I either find a job or find myself in a grave."

The Italian turned to face me again, his expression reflecting that he was simultaneously impressed and horrified.

"Now that I think about it," he replied, "I do have a job for you, not that many people capable of handling the situation it imposes, but you seem like you could do anything for a better life."

"I can agree to that," I say readily.

"Follow me."

I turned my back on the world that took everything away from me and followed him to a back room that seemed to be nothing out of the ordinary.

"What is your name, mister?" the Italian asked.

"Carl Smith."

"Pleasure to meet you Mr. Smith," he replied as I passed by a storage room, its contents obscured by darkness, and then a small but adequate kitchen.

"We have arrived at our destination!" Italian said as he opens a door to a room even darker than the rooms before it.

I glanced around for a moment, but it was too dark to discern anything recognizable.

"Stand here while I get the lights on," he told me, slowly backing out of the room.

"Why must I stand in there, can I not stand out here in the hall where I can see?" I asked, as he turned back to me, trying to reassert himself in the situation.

"Mr. Smith, do you want the job or not? It's going to be obvious what you need to do once I have the lights on. Now please wait a moment."

I hesitated briefly before realizing that this may be the last opportunity I have.

I conceded and walked into the desolate room, staring into an abyss of nothingness.

"I'll be right back," he said as he hurried away.

The moment I turned my eye from the halls of light I came from and into the space of nothingness in which I now dwelt, I heard the door behind me slam as hard as my heart began to slam against the cage of my ribs.

"Hey!" I screamed, fearing I had walked into my own death bed.

"Sorry. mister, I forgot to put the door stopper down, it appears that it is locked. Let me go get my keys." The Italian's voice is muffled through the door.

"Hurry up!" My reply was in the form of a loud scream.

I waited, and I waited, and I waited… The ticking of the clock outside echoes into the interior; the only sensation I could detect in liminal arena I occupied.

"Hello, hello, HELLOOOO!" I shouted abruptly, my vocals shaking as much as my arms as I began to slam my fist on the door. I hear nothing on the outside, silence replies, the ticking ceases as my last line of hope abruptly ceases as I now stood in complete solitude.

Then, out of nothingness, the room begins to shake, like I was in a salt-shaker seasoning a giant's meal. I quickly dropped onto the floor, grabbing on to an unknown metal object. I began to hear what sounds like a mixture of fireworks and a dragon breathing fire.  "You see that chair, get into it and hold tight. It's going to be a bumpy ride!" The Italian yells as the room's lights finally awaken, revealing a room covered in multiply colored metals, with lights flashing colors of gold, red, and blue.

I quickly planted myself into the chair, and instantly I was sucked into it like a magnet as the room suddenly flies off like a plane. As the force increased, my body felt as though it was slowly morphing into the chair. The room's speed increased more and more, shifting left and right, up and down. I felt as if I was inside a ball getting hit back and forth by Babe Ruth and Lou Gehrig. The motions were far too much for my already bridled body, my eyelids closed in, and I once again fell into darkness.

## Chapter III: A Yankee in King Tom's Court

I was woken by a strain of light beaming between the two curtains in front of me. I heard a man talking beyond, spouting words I could not understand as I tried to find a way out of this chair. I tapped a white button on the chair, which immediately dropped me of its tight grasp. I fell to the ground, still dazzled and confused. After a minute or so I managed to pick myself up, slowly creeping up into the crack of light ahead. The man's words began to sound more comprehensible as I listened.

"Tonight's show is going to be *Quantumtastic* as usual; I have a special guest hailing straight from the Great Depression!!!" the man announces as the crowd gasps with intrigue.

"Now, before we start, should you like to learn more about this very depressing time in the history of Old America, scan this expo code through your E-Glasses. It will take you to our immersive history VR museum, where you can experience history in the comfort of your own home. Data rates apply, see your Eigo rep for details. And now, without further ado, here is tonight's guest, Mr. Smith!" the voice from beyond said, and I heard an abrupt roar of claps as the curtains in front of me part to reveal a massive crowd of people, each having a pair of visors of changing color, wearing clothes seemingly out of the futurist artwork I began to see once the '30s began, being overweight seemed like a universal factor among them as they all hovered on individual chairs keeping their lop sided bodies afloat.

I stood there in pure shock, as rock solid as those two fellows in the corner of the bar were. The clapping slowly started to fade, being exchanged with a few giggles as I look back and forth at the crowd, not knowing if I was stuck in coma or stolen by Martians.

"Well, are you going to come up and chat, Mr. Smith?" The man in the front of a levitating desk asked. He was dressed in a suit that kept changing color, ever changing as if by whim, his face and massive body that looks perfectly defined, his hair like a topiary bush at the City Garden, seemingly cut perfectly into shape.

He waved his hand like a circus ringmaster, twirling around his palm as I slowly walked across the stage, holding on to the glass wall behind me. I looked outside at night sky in which a large planet, covered with red and blue, was attracting what I could only describe as warships sailing in the dark waters of space. I had the impulse to scream until my throat exploded and to run back into the room, but my will seems to have been subdued, my body acts against my mind as I made it into a levitating chair opposite who I suppose is Quan-Tom.

"Mr. Smith, on a scale of one to one hundred, how are you feeling today?" Tom says, as lights in the shape of numbers appeared in front of me.

I respond, "Where am I?" as I tussle in my mind for control over my own body.

"They always say that. Well, Mr. Smith, this is History Retold with you host Quan-Tom, broadcasting from the year—" he pauses as he points to the crowd, who respond with a roar of "THREE THOUSAND FORTY!"

"That is right, we are living the sixth industrial revolution, which has brought us the trans material clothing, the Infibite data chips, and most importantly the Peepo pill!" he says as the crowd erupts in laughter, and a few lights appear showing what I could only assume to be the items he just mentioned, looking like a combination of moving pictures and the billboards I would see on Broadway.

"Can I have some water?" I asked bleakly, feeling as though my lips are being programmed like I am a puppet as the crowd continues to laugh away.

"Sure thing!" He says as he shows me an empty cup, he then pretends as though he is capturing something in it, guiding it through the air. He put a metallic cap on the cup, then removed it, revealing it to be filled with water.

I took a sip from the cup, feeling refreshed by this water appearing out of nowhere. "How did you do that?" I asked.

He holds up the metallic cap again for me and the audience to see. "This little bad boy is the Elementogade 400, each sold separately, cup not included!" As he speaks, another light appears in front of the crowd, shouting BUY NOW, ONLY 39,999.99!

"But this show isn't about this *boring* century," he continued, "It's about learning and discovering the past of our fathers and learning gripping stories of the struggles of Earth prior to the Great Disturbance. Now, tell us about yourself, Mr. Smith" Tom said.

"Well, I was born in 1904 in New York." I say, as I slowly give up control, quickly submitting to the enemy I do not know.

Tom interjects, "NYC, I love New York City, the Tentagirls at Empirical Hyper Club are something else, let me tell you." The crowd laughs and whistles. "I once had one of those tentacles stuck all around on me, I guess she was a newbie. Always bring protection," he added with a wink.

He turned back to me, "What was your childhood like?"

"My family where fairly poor, my father was a laborer at the Smith and Co Factory and a serial gambler on the side. The moment we had an extra dollar to spare it was slowly consumed by his ever-growing sin. I had to inevitably assume the mantal of the man of the house and began work all throughout town.

"I worked as a paper boy, a salesman, even took up work in a textile plant. I worked like this for a few years, until luck bumped into me, literally, as the owner of Mr. Butcher, who owned a general store right next door to my home nearly walked straight into me.

"He instantly reckoned the once little boy who would always come into his store and get groceries for his family and struck up an hour-long conversation between the two of us. Long story short he needed some help and offered he a job at his store, and not with a second more I accepted his offer." I was forced to say, my words seemingly pushed out of my voice like I was possessed, no longer corresponding with the truth.

"Now, for those who don't know what a cashier is, it was a job people in the ancient days had, when items weren't instantly shipped through the tube. You actually had to go to a store." Tom said, as though I was an Ancient Babylonian.

I continued "The next few years I was living in paradise, managing that wonderful shop. I saved enough to buy a beautiful apartment just west of the store that could fit my whole family in. I got married to my love of my life, Elizabeth, and had my little Susanne on the way. I'd spend the weekends watching plays on Broadway and listening to jazz on $52^{nd}$."

"You had to travel to watch a show! Today you simply say, 'show!'" Tom shouted as his googles lights flicker. "I don't know why these people just didn't stay home," he said, pointing he eyes towards the crowd of floaters.

"Because we love you, Tom!" One floater shouted in excitement of his mere presence.

"If I stated my opinion about these people I would be cancelled on every broadcast network east of Andromeda." He says as they continue to laugh, never ceasing to be entertained.

"My life hit its peak at the birth of my daughter," I explain, "As the most important moment of my life was manifesting, it seemed as though I reached the peak of a mountain, then seemingly fell down the steep slopes instantaneously as my Elizabeth passed on during childbirth.  Two years later, the day that will be remembered for centuries, Black Thursday, occurred. Everything I had worked for vanished overnight as the market crashed as hard as my father on a Friday night." My controller says as the whole crowd begins to laugh and spin in their levitating chairs, making light of the darkest moment in my life, as I try to spit out a tear drop to signal the monumental stress I was in.

"From then on, I only had me, Susanne, and the shirt on my back. I had to seek refuge in the Hooverville slums set up in the east villages, jumping from job to job, only for their pay to dry up, and for yet another layoff. The rest of my family abandoned me and my daughter and headed westward, to the sunset."

"Very interesting. So, you said you have a daughter?"

"Yes, my little Susanne, she is only seven, but she has the smarts of a seventeen-year-old. She learned quick, she would help me at the cash register, being able to manage the store on her own while I ran for supplies." I state, though the truth is that she would help me stock the shelves at the library.

"My kiddo can't even brush his teeth properly, and he's sixty! Kids these days. Gotta ships him back to 1930, that will teach him a lesson. Your life seems like a sad, depressing tale—" Tom turned to address the audience, "This man's situation in life perfectly demonstrates that the policies that Fredi McNary is pushing for will destroy the galactic economy as we know it! Do you want to end up like Mr. Smith over here?" he asked them, then to me as an aside, "No offense."

He spoke in an increasingly arrogant manner as the floaters shook their heads, "I thought not. Mr. Smith, it has been a pleasure talking with you, you are such a fascinating character indeed! I would love to give you a gift, Mr. Smith, straight from the heart!" he exclaims as beams of red light in the form of a heart sprinkle from his chest.

"What is the gift you have for me?" I asked in a state of bewilderment.

"Well, I don't think you would like to return to those dark days of the 1930s. That is why I am giving you this all-expense paid luxury home!" He yells, showing off a model of a luxury home in front of the crowd as a weight instantly seems to fly off my shoulders while the crowd cheers on and on. "Welcome to the Thirty First Century, where all dreams are possible!"

I feel as if I am slipping in and out of consciousness. "Am I in a dream?" I ask, grasping at any hope of normalcy.

Tom instantly slapped me across the face and a rush of blood flowed like water through my veiny pipes back into my brain.
"Does that feel real, ha, ha, ha!"

"This can't be real!" I shouted.

"You forgot that we are in the age of possibility, with our expansion into the stars we have billions of new acres of free real estate, and robots do most of the work anyway." Tom says.

"But what about my daughter, I just can't leave her?" I say as worry quickly covers my mind.

"You ever heard the saying that you leave the best part of the Pizza for last? Ladies and gentlemen, say hello to Little Susanne!" he announced triumphantly as I turn around and see my little beauty running towards me.

"Daddy!" she says as she jumps like a panther into my arms.

"Oh, my little Susanne, how I have missed you so much. I have great news, this won-derful man is giving us a house and everything needed for us to live a great life, no more struggle no more pain, we can truly live happily ever after." I explained and hugged her with bony arms, certain that we were finally leaving a life a pain and misery behind.

I shook Toms hand as ballons rose from the ground all round me.

"Welcome to the Thirty-First, where all dreams are possible!" Susanne and I are escorted to the back of the stage by what appears to be robots like the ones in Metropolis.

I heard Tom speak one last time. "Up next, an exclusive with a privateer who aided in the capture of the ferocious Blackbeard, after the break!" His announcement is followed by music that my old ears could barely comprehend. I turned my head away from the stage and in an instant a cloud of gas quickly ingulfed my face, "This is for your safety, Mr. Smith," says Tom, and I fainted into black once more.

## Chapter IV: Paradise Regained Again

"Aaaahhhh!" I shouted as my eyes opened to a brightly lit bedroom. I was in a bed as soft as a marshmallow. I quickly woke the rest of my body and slugged out of bed, pain instantly rushed into my head as I quickly rested it upon my palm, an excruciating pain that felt like pins and needles in my brain.

My mind recovered a few moments later as I began turning in circles, feeling both awe and unease at the room I now occupied, the walls painted a pleasurable peach color, and the timber floorboards marvelously coated with the finest of gold. I looked out one of the vast picture windows and beheld a green valley with acres of grass flourishing beneath the sun's brilliant rays. I could see other mansions such as this in the distance.

"Am I in heaven?" I asked myself out loud, my brain incapable of merely holding such a question in my mind.

I walked down the stairs, and I began to explore the house, mesmerized by the gold all around glinting like a golden sea. I made it downstairs, following the sound of falling water. The noise led me past multiple rooms, and I was overwhelmed by the pure quantity of material that had been dropped on me.

I soon found myself in the kitchen and there I met a young lady; her golden hair flowing from the winds sweeping through the window, her body perfectly proportioned, her face pure and pale. The moment I entered the room she looks up and her cute little mouth turns into a grin as though she seen one of those Muscle Men from the circus.

"Hi, I was wondering when you would finally wake up."

"Hello," I replied, my face showing my confusion, "Who might you be?"

"I'm Samantha, your house maid." she says in an even more confused manner.

"Right, right. Samantha, how are you today?" I ask as I steady myself by placing my hand on a nearby cabinet.

"Better since you're here now! I nearly got the dishes done. Is there anything else you need me to do?"

"Yes, can you tell me where Susanne is?" I asked, anxious to see my little angel once more.

"In her room."

"Right… which is *that* way?" I say as I point my finger down the hall I came out of.

"No," she clarified, "I meant, *that* way. Up the stairs and to the right."

"Right, right. Sorry, last night was took a toll on me, to say the least."

"I'll make sure were not up all night tonight," she says with a twinkle in her eyes and a subtle blush.

"Right, right, goodbye for now." I retrace the path I had come, completely dumbfounded by the conversation I just had.

I walked up the stairs and into Susanne's room, where I found her sleeping like a little angel, although this struck me as strange, seeing as she's usually up bright and early, far before I am.      "Little Susanne, wake up," I said as I gently shake her shoulders.

"Daddy, I want to sleep." she says as she pulls her blanket over her face.

"Susanne, what has gotten into you? Look outside, there are kids running around out there," I tell her, pointing out the window to a group of children playing in the valley.

She instantly slingshots out of bed and in front of the window. "My friends are out there. Yay!" she hollers as she runs out of her room and down the stairs in her pajamas. I swiftly followed, yelling, "Get you clothes on first." But I quickly lose sight of her in this large mausoleum.

I spent the next few hours wandering around the grand house, examining every square inch as it all seemed intensely mesmerizing. "Why would someone give this to me for free?" I wondered aloud.

There are a few objects I do not understand the use of at all, such as the large black box in the kitchen, filled with the finest foods I had ever seen. The interior was cool, so I could only suppose it was some sort of refrigeration mechanism.

In my room there sat a flat, black tablet upon my desk, with a small little mouse-like contraption connected to it. I tapped upon the mouse only for lights blasted from its face. The images startle my curiosity and I saw forms I could not even begin to understand. It did not help that none of the images included words… very strange indeed.

Deciding to head outside and meet some of my new neighbors, I tried to find where all my clothes were.

"Samantha!" I yelled.

"I'm in the laundry room." Samantha replied, her voice echoing from far away.

I tried to orient myself as to her location. "What room?"

"The laundry room."

I decided to just follow her voice. I found her downstairs, reaching into a strange machine.

"Oh hey, can you pass me some clothes?" I asked as she pulls herself upright, holding an armload of what appear to be men's clothing.

"Do you want to walk around in wet socks?" she asks.

"I prefer dry socks." I said, as she begins to giggle away.

"They'll be dry soon," she told me, transferring the items to yet another machine, "I'll let you know."

I waited a little more, wandering down to the basement, but there was nothing noteworthy in its empty corridors.

I stumbled into a bathroom containing, to my relief, a functioning toilet and bath, an immeasurably superior upgrade from the bucket and river I had been acquainted with.

I looked into the mirror to the right of me, my face looking sharper than ever, a far cry from the low-level stock I was relegated to.

My face was white and clear and freshly shaved; my hair was cut and seemingly darker and more defined than ever.

"Your clothes are ready!" Samantha's voice carries through the empty corridors.

I turned my head towards the sound of her voice, but for the briefest of moments, at the bottom of the doorway, I saw a bizarre being with one large black eye held by a long cord.

"What the Hell!" I exclaimed as it instantly retreated from sight.

I quickly followed, only for there to be no sign of its presence.

Samantha, hearing my scream, rushed into the room. "What is the matter?" she asked, clutching my now dried socks.

"I saw some creature peeping at me in the bathroom." I explained, glancing at all corners of the room.

"You must be seeing things; I had the bathroom in my sight. You were looking in the mirror and I only saw your perfect body," she said, seemingly trying to seduce me away from the situation as she rubs my shoulder.

"I... ah... I'm... ah..." Words eluded me; she was like Circe trying to seduce Odysseus. "I ah, need to go out and take a breather." I said as I tried to grab a hold of my socks, but her hands were faster than mine.

"You're going to have to chase me, big boy," she laughed as I reluctantly pursued her.

She hopped like a bunny up the stairs then ran like a cougar down the halls. My slow body couldn't keep up as I quickly lost sight of her. I followed the trail of laughter and found her dress on the floor in front of my room.

I opened the door to visuals of pure pleasure, a picture so perfect that not even a painting from the greatest Renaissance painters could compare. As a gentleman, I'll not tell you what transpired in the moments thereafter.

I woke up yet again later that day with Samantha's thin arms wrapped around my bare chest. I glanced at the clock near my bed, the arms indicating that it was 4:04. I slid out of bed, trying not to wake my seductress and sat there in silence for a moment, pondering the stunning valley in which I now dwelt.

Samantha snuck up behind me and placed her hand on my shoulder. "Beautiful, isn't it?"

"It is indeed, it looks like a scene from Mark Twain book." I replied as I looked across the horizon.

This innocent comment caused something within Samantha to snap, as though I said some great blasphemy or forbidden statement. Her eyes turned red as she grabbed the back of my shirt and tossed me like a javelin into the wall, despite her small stature.

My impact with the wall was so intense that I flew right through it and landed in a black hallway with transparent glass looking into my room. A few strange fat beings, floating entities, stared down at me as though I was some beast in a zoo.

Alarms sounding, Samantha pounced in front of me, and as she looked down at me with bloodshot eyes, the black crystal-eyed being I had seen earlier slithered around me, griping its tight metal snakelike scales around my body like a python about to feast on its prey. The beast's eye opened, spewing a cloud of green gas that quickly subdued my body.

"You are by far the most incompetent piece of low life trash I had ever laid my eyes on! Do you know the consequences of bringing the ideas that old bum out into our world? The Council will not allow such a matter to gain any foothold."

Her words were still ringing in my ears and even before they faded, I wake up, unaware of the passage of time, feeling that I am in an endless cycle of reincarnation. This time I was in a cold grey room, covered with machines of daunting design, like metal gargoyles looking down upon me from their perch, arms sticking out of them with their hands replaced with saws and screws.

A pair walked into the room; one is a slender being, covered in a garb I could only describe as a mix of a plague doctor, a Klansman, and a native as he is escorted by what appears to be his handler. This man wore a suit ever changing in color, with spiked black glasses, and his hair cut out like the bushes of the city garden, his face appearing in the spectrum of my memory, though I cannot recall where.

They saw that I was awake and I tried to yell, but had a large metal and rubber blocks my mouth, and my body was seemingly glued to the chair.

"You didn't even apply enough synthozide to knock him out long enough for the procedure! Damn it, we have no time at all, we must get this operation done now, but if he gets a Kindo worm in his mind, you're going to pay the loss of his life with yours, little Wiggit," the man said as he placed a dome atop my head. "You're one pain in the ass, you know that? I guess that's one reason why your kind ceased to exist, the bigger fish in the sea noticed didn't put up with that. Now you will become just like one of us," he said as he took off his glasses, staring directly into my soul with eyes of uncanny design, both black and white, big and small, changing in shape and style in an instant.

"Start the monobot!" He yelled at the doctor as the machine began to turn like a tornado while I looked up. The blades pierced my skull and the machine turns ever faster as I try to yell out in agony, though my tongue is held by the machine. The top of my head is ripped from my person, though the machine seems to be keeping my body alive.

"You put in the coordinates for the cerebrum and the cortex, and then you place the blockers here, not at the hippocampus, so much for wasting the medical schools time and resources.." he continued speaking even as I felt the alien object being placed within my brain. My body went numb; my eyes occupied as I lost control over my own body, fleeing into the confines of my own inner monologue.

## Epilogue

Who is Carl Smith?

To the people that lived in 1934 New York he was a kind soul down on his luck that one day dropped out of existence, like many others taken back by the fruits of the time.

To a little girl named Susanne, he is a loving father who now can only cry, and cry, and cry at what will be her conclusion as she seems alone in this alien world.

To his captors he is a vessel for profit, an attraction of a bygone era, indifferent to the mental renditions as they gain near absolute control over him.

To himself he is but a walking corpse, a being with a mind, but one cut off to its psychical form, only able to watch from the prison of his own thoughts.

# Another Day, Another Dollar
by Shawn Fairchild

*"The Moonscorched are born of moonlight. They do not mean harm—but to see them is to be arrested, and those who linger in the lunar light become one of them."*

When I awoke, I was drenched in sweat—thick, black, and clinging like oil. It coated me, seeped into me. I couldn't scrub it off.

Before I recount what I saw, let me tell you how the shadows danced across my room, how doom took on scent and shape, and how those weightless images pinned me down long after they vanished, turning me into a prisoner within my own body. The lights were off.

The only light filling the room was cast by Selene—her silver hair pouring through the window, began to impart strange life to the objects strewn about my room.

The clutter—clothes, furniture, stray belongings—morphed into shadows. Figures. Each began moving with eerie purpose. The first moved slowly, heavily. Its limbs dragged like soaked cloth; each step deliberate and measured as if it were trying to walk its way out of a decision. It paced back and forth, halting just long enough to look at me. It had no face—no features at all. It resembled an undressed wooden mannequin, the kind painters would use, reliant entirely on moonlight for animation. It was composed utterly of shadow.

I was terrified by its rhythm.

I couldn't tell how long it had been pacing, or how long it would continue. But I knew this kind of pacing: it was the nervous kind, the kind you do just before a decision, or just after one that cannot be undone. Another crouched, long-limbed and skeletal, flipping through invisible pages strewn on the floor. Its fingers twitched with manic precision, searching for something it couldn't name. When it finally raised its head, I saw no face—only a keyhole where one should be. From deep within it came a sound: a faint whisper just loud enough that it made me want to get closer to understand it.

Another sat at the foot of my bed, perfectly still except for its face. It wore a wide, unnatural grin that split all the way to its ears. Its inky black teeth were flat and countless, like a shark's. Hands folded politely, it leaned in. The smile widened, but the rest of it didn't move an inch, as though the smile existed independent of the body that bore it. Another stood by the closet. It opened and closed the door endlessly. Open. Close. Open. Close. With each repetition, its form blurred, becoming less human. Wind from the windows leaked in and blew into its head, the wind intoned a looping chant: "again, again, again."

Another knelt with its face pressed to the floor, arms spread in supplication. It made no sound. But when the moonlight touched it, its spine began to arch—slowly, unnaturally—like a bowstring drawn by invisible hands. One stood in the far corner, a cord trailing from its ear into the dark. It mimed the action of answering a rotary phone, again and again, though the phone never rang. Each time it lifted the receiver, its jaw unhinged further, until it creaked and cracked with the strain. Another walked in place, its legs a blur, its upper body perfectly still. It produced a low whirring hum, like an old printer. Its mouth moved in silent apologies or reports, and its eyes stared forward blank, waiting, resigned.

These were the shadows that haunted me.

And now, the dream. I was wandering through what seemed like endless alleys, searching. For what, I didn't know. But I knew that if I saw it, it would reveal itself. The architecture was strange—dreamlike, almost indescribable, though it bore the fingerprints of human laborers. I could never find my way. For every dusty corridor I entered, five more branched out.

The labyrinth grew as I walked. The walls pulsed as if they breathed, they shifted as if they lived. There was something organic about this place. And the moonlight. As Selene's glow poured in from some impossible height, the labyrinth twisted inward. Its walls folded, merged, tightened, squeezing me tightly and when the pressure was nigh unbearable, right when I should have awoke, I was spat out before a door. The corridor was a gullet, narrow and wet. The bricks flaked like calloused dead skin, and Selene's glow revealed all of it to me. She was emitting a low hum, concentrating herself on the door alone, anything else I could make out was her being unable to contain her power. The air was thick with time, the atmosphere more akin to a morgue.

And there it was: the door.

Painted a sick, swampy green—like something dredged up rather than built. On its face, a sign. A plea? A lure? "HELP WANTED — Inquire Within."

The letters looked handwritten, but not by any human hand. Too smooth. Too practiced. And yet, they bled into each other—as if something had mimicked human writing in desperation, without truly understanding it. Was it an invitation to apply? Or an initiation—to become part of whatever waited inside?

The frame was too solid for this melting world. An anchor. Untouched by time or rot. It had not merely been placed there—it had always been there. And it had been waiting. For me, or someone like me. For anyone foolish enough to believe what lay beyond it might be meaningful.

I didn't knock. I was too afraid.

But I turned the handle. As the door creaked open, the moonlight behind me died. Inside: darkness, and motion, but now Selene was directly above, super-massive in her appearance, she nearly blinded me. The roof of this building was a massive dome, totally transparent, just behind it where she stood.

There was nothing but moon above, there was no darkness or night behind her, there were no stars to be seen, just moon. In the room itself, shadows, smiling as they worked. Some paced in sterile offices, moving through routines beneath Selene's crystalline glow. Others, faceless, filed endless stacks of paper. A few knelt in silence, as if in prayer.

At the center of the room, where moon's beam was freely concentrated, sat one more scorched than all the rest.

He grinned widely and deliberately and unlike the others, his expression wasn't hollow. He was content. Radiant. Absolutely immersed in what he had become. He reached out his hand, and I reached out mine.

The moment we touched, his hand wrapped firmly around mine, and he yanked me forward with the force of something rabid.

That's when I awoke, slicked in that black, oil-like sweat. But as you know, many things followed me out. Now I cannot sleep. The thoughts of them, the moonscorched, haunt every corner of my house. I see their shapes in reflections, hear their movements behind closed doors. They are with me, still, and I have no hope of escaping.

And yet, the most-scorched one is nowhere to be found. I am the one keeping him around. I can't help but wonder about him. He was happy. Not trapped: chosen. That grin he held never ceased, the way he sat in her glow was as a child in its mother's breast. Selene's heat was warming us all that night, but he was the only one cuddling into it, bearing it, extending her light. He was like a magnifying glass for her bright light. When she shone on him, he reflected it out two-fold. The shadows were unlike him: he embraced what he was doing, they were just doing to be doing. I don't know what I stand to gain from writing this. Perhaps nothing. But I do know this: that door is still out there, basking in the moon's glow. The labyrinth still shifts, hunting for dreamers. And that most-moonscorched man is still waiting in the center of her glow for someone else to answer the call: HELP WANTED—Inquire Within.

# Profoundly Alone
## by Erik F. Hill

**Part One: A Flickering Invitation**

A flashing red neon sign buzzed like a trapped insect above a storefront window on a forgotten street corner in South Park, Los Angeles. It was the kind of urban landscape that seemed perpetually on the brink of revival—graffiti-covered walls sandwiched between shiny new apartments and shuttered store fronts. The sign blinked erratically, its half-lit message an ambiguous beacon that drew us closer.

My smoking hot girlfriend, Lauren, stood at my side, gripping the handlebars of her red beach cruiser. A single-speed she'd bought from a street vendor on Vermont Avenue. She wore a simple black and yellow sun dress that barely reached midthigh. No underwear tonight—her impulsive choice, enticingly reckless, though perhaps impractical given the night's promise. Her mischievous smile made it clear she knew exactly what effect she was having on me.

"Think this is it?" she asked, squinting at the ambiguous storefront.

"It has to be," I replied, glancing down at the crumpled flyer I'd pulled from my pocket:

THE ALONE EXPERIENCE: An Existential Haunting
Help Wanted, Inquire Within.

The flyer promised terror, introspection, confrontation of fears—all woven into a tapestry of existential dread. We'd found it taped inconspicuously to a lamppost near our Koreatown rental house, sandwiched among faded ads for yard sales and amateur psychic readings.

Lauren squeezed my hand, her voice dipping into a conspiratorial whisper. "Do you think we just walk in?"

"Only one way to find out."

We stepped toward the storefront. Beyond the grimy window, shadows moved inside, vague outlines shifting behind tattered curtains. Yet the door wouldn't yield, locked tight. I pushed harder, rattling it briefly in frustration.

"Locked?" Lauren asked, amused.

I stared up at the blinking sign, reconsidering. "Maybe this isn't the entrance at all."

She looked around, eyes landing on the darkened parking lot beside the building. It was fenced, a rusted chain-link barrier crowned with spirals of barbed wire. "I bet it's in the back. Through there."

I eyed the fence skeptically. "Seems sketchy."

Lauren grinned, a glimmer of daring dancing in her eyes. "Everything fun is sketchy."

With adrenaline suddenly pulsing, we wheeled our bikes toward the fence, gravel crunching beneath our shoes. We heaved the bicycles upward, metal spokes scraping against wire, until they toppled clumsily into the shadowed lot on the other side. A brief moment of doubt flashed through my mind—but Lauren was already climbing. Her dress lifted dangerously, revealing pale skin in flashes under the dim streetlight. I chuckled softly, partly in admiration and partly in disbelief at our recklessness.

"Be careful," I called, unable to keep amusement out of my voice.

She landed gracefully, then quickly adjusted the hem of her dress, eyes flashing with excitement. "Your turn."

Scaling the fence, I felt the familiar thrill of rule breaking I'd chased my entire life. My feet hit gravel; we were inside. But the parking lot offered nothing but cracked asphalt, rusted dumpsters, and the unsettling stillness of abandoned spaces.

"Maybe it's not through here," I murmured, disappointment edging my voice.

Lauren's smile never wavered. "Keep going."

On the opposite side of the lot stood another fence—taller, more imposing. Without hesitation, we repeated our ritual: bikes hurled gracelessly over wire and metal, scraping loudly enough to alert anyone nearby, and another tense climb.

As Lauren scaled again, her dress fluttered, fully revealing herself this time, unapologetic and unabashed. Her laughter punctuated the silence, a thrilling sound echoing off brick walls. I followed, my heart hammering.

Emerging into a narrow alleyway, we stopped, breathless and exhilarated.

Before us stood a solitary steel door, illuminated only by a bare yellow bulb dangling from frayed wiring. On it, scrawled in stark white paint:

HELP WANTED, INQUIRE WITHIN

Lauren turned to me, eyes wide with exhilaration, pupils dilated by anticipation and the remnants of cocaine we'd shared earlier, back in the warmth of our Koreatown room. "You ready?"

I nodded, pulse quickening again. "Absolutely."

She grasped the handle, metal cool against her skin, and pulled the heavy door open with a creak that echoed down the shadowy corridor beyond. Cold, damp air washed over us, carrying a faintly metallic scent.

We exchanged a final glance—a look loaded with excitement, desire, and the deliciously uncertain promise of fear. We stepped inside together, allowing the door to slam shut behind us with an ominous boom.

A voice crackled from hidden speakers, distorted yet chillingly intimate: "You've arrived alone. Only in isolation will you truly find yourselves."

Lauren pressed closer, her breath warm against my neck. She whispered, teasing, defiant, "Think they'll separate us?"

I squeezed her hand, smiling despite the sudden chill. "They can try."

Somewhere deep within the darkness ahead, laughter echoed—a brittle sound devoid of joy, sending shivers down my spine.

Our existential haunting had begun.


**Part Two: Separation Anxiety**

We stood shoulder to shoulder in pitch-black darkness, the air stagnant and heavy. Our fingers intertwined instinctively. My heart pounded in my chest, a drumbeat of anticipation and dread pulsing through every nerve.

A thick velvet curtain hung behind us, a barrier we hadn't noticed when we entered. From somewhere beyond it, footsteps echoed softly—slow, deliberate steps approaching with predatory patience.

Lauren's grip tightened. Her breathing quickened, the warmth of her bare shoulder pressed firmly against mine. "Here it comes," she whispered, voice tinged with an excitement that belied any fear.

I nodded silently, the gesture invisible in the oppressive gloom.

The curtain rustled abruptly, breaking the silence. A hand, impossibly strong and sudden, seized my shoulder, wrenching me backward through the heavy velvet. Lauren's hand slipped from mine.

Before I could protest, a blinding white LED flashlight blasted into my eyes. The intensity of it drilled into my retinas, obliterating vision and thought. Pain flared sharply, and I squinted uselessly against the intrusion. The world became nothing but white-hot pulses.

A gravelly voice rasped into my ear, intimate yet menacingly detached. "Alone. Always alone."

I gasped, shielding my eyes, disoriented and furious at myself for allowing vulnerability. Just as abruptly as the light appeared, it was extinguished, plunging me once again into absolute darkness.

"Lauren?" My voice cracked, echoing faintly into emptiness.

Silence.

I stretched out my hands, fingers reaching blindly. I felt nothing but stale air and empty space. My stomach tightened. An anxious pang shot through me, unexpectedly fierce. We were apart, deliberately isolated.

The promise of the flyer returned, mockingly precise: Existential Haunting.

I took a tentative step forward, arms outstretched, guided purely by instinct. I stumbled slightly, fumbling for balance. My fingers brushed against damp concrete walls, the texture rough, cold, and unforgiving. A corridor? I traced the wall's contour carefully, moving forward in hesitant steps, every sound magnified by the silence.

"Lauren?" I whispered again, louder this time, strained urgency coating my words. Only my own breathing replied.

My hands slid cautiously along the surface, scraping across peeling paint and crumbling brick. The floor was uneven beneath my feet, gritty debris scattering softly with each cautious step.

Without sight, other senses sharpened dramatically—every creak, every echo intensified my paranoia. Each sound became a distorted chorus of imagined threats.

Suddenly, a faint whisper echoed nearby, too soft to discern clearly. I froze, straining desperately to make sense of the murmuring words, but they melted away into silence as quickly as they arrived.

A cool breeze brushed my cheek, carrying the stale scent of dust and mold. My heartbeat raced faster, the sound filling my ears. I felt deeply, intensely alone. A realization crawled into my consciousness, gnawing at the edges of rationality: this experience was designed to amplify isolation, to magnify existential dread.

"Just keep moving," I muttered aloud, trying to reassure myself as my anxiety built. Lauren would be experiencing this too—alone, vulnerable in that dangerously provocative dress, navigating her own unseen horrors. My chest tightened at the thought, my protectiveness heightened by helplessness.

I moved forward with greater urgency, determined to navigate whatever challenge this bizarre experiment presented. My fingers trailed a rough edge—a doorframe. Hesitantly, I pushed inward. Hinges groaned. I stepped through.

Suddenly, something soft brushed my arm. I recoiled sharply, adrenaline spiking. Fabric? The curtain again? No—a different texture entirely. Carefully, trembling, I reached out again, exploring cautiously. Cloth, soft and dense, hung in heavy drapes from above.

Then it dawned: these were garments, hundreds of them. A narrow maze of hanging clothes formed a claustrophobic passage. An absurd thought arose—help wanted; inquire within—was this a metaphor, an existential job interview of sorts, lost in a wardrobe of identities we choose?

I pushed aside a heavy wool coat and moved deeper into the textile labyrinth, every step obscured by layers of musty clothing brushing against my skin. Each piece carried its own faint aroma—cologne, perfume, sweat, smoke—ghostly remnants of lives previously inhabited.

Then, without warning, fingers closed tightly around my wrist.

I spun, startled, heart hammering. "Lauren?"

The hand held firm, silent, leading me onward with confident urgency. My breath came in shallow bursts as I was pulled through the final curtain of fabric, stepping once more into open space.

A dim yellow bulb flickered to life overhead.

My captor—a young woman with striking green eyes—stared calmly into my startled expression, her grip still firm. Her face was blank, expressionless.

"Sit," she commanded softly, gesturing toward a lone wooden chair beneath the light.

My pulse still raced, but I complied, dropping heavily onto the creaking seat. "Who are—" I began, but she raised a single finger sharply, demanding silence.

She leaned in close, eyes boring into mine, voice barely audible yet impossibly clear: "What frightens you most—being alone, or finding out who you really are when nobody's watching?"

I hesitated, my tongue suddenly thick, unsure how honest to be. "I…I'm not sure."

She smiled enigmatically, a faint flicker of amusement dancing across her lips. "You will be."

She stepped back abruptly, vanishing into shadow, leaving me once again alone under the flickering bulb, heart still thundering.           A distant scream pierced the silence—Lauren's voice unmistakably, threaded with fear yet undeniably tinged with excitement. My gut churned, torn between protective panic and an electric thrill.

I took a breath, steeling myself for whatever came next, knowing that somewhere nearby, Lauren navigated her own harrowing introspection, dress lifted by some unseen current, defiant and exposed.

We had willingly surrendered control, embracing vulnerability and chaos, trusting blindly in an experience designed explicitly to terrify and liberate.

I rose slowly, stepping forward into darkness, the uncertainty now strangely comforting. Whatever lay ahead, we'd chosen this—to confront the hidden rooms of ourselves, and ultimately, each other.

We had asked for this.


**Part Three: Channeling Shadows**

I pressed forward, my breathing shallow and cautious as I navigated another dim, narrow corridor. The faint yellow illumination faded quickly behind me, plunging my surroundings into ink-black silence once again.

My thoughts drifted uneasily to Lauren. Somewhere nearby she, too, navigated her own twisting pathways—fearful, exhilarated, vulnerable. The soft shuffle of footsteps occasionally echoed beyond the walls, disembodied and distant, reminding me we were never truly alone here, yet irrevocably separated.

Ahead, a thin outline of pale amber light seeped through the crack of a doorframe. My pulse quickened. Hand trembling, I reached out, gripping the cold brass handle and pushed inward. Hinges squealed softly as I stepped into a dimly lit room, the door clicking shut behind me.

An elderly man sat alone at a small wooden table, backlit by the soft flicker of a single antique lamp. Shadows danced gently along the weathered surface of his lined, expressionless face. A heavy silence stretched between us, interrupted only by the faint hum of electricity from unseen machinery somewhere deep inside the building.

"Sit," he said, his voice low and gravelly, surprisingly gentle.

I complied without question, sliding onto the worn wooden chair opposite him. His eyes, watery yet piercingly sharp, regarded me with quiet patience. Something in their intensity stirred a sense of unease deep in my chest.

"You're troubled," he murmured after a long moment. His gaze softened almost imperceptibly. "Everyone who seeks this place is troubled."

I swallowed, hesitating. "I suppose."

He leaned forward slightly, clasping his weathered hands atop the table. Long, pale fingers interlaced slowly, knuckles bony beneath translucent skin. "But your trouble is special," he continued. "You fear loss. More than anything else, you fear losing what you love."

I shifted uncomfortably, suddenly aware of the weight of his words. "Everyone fears that."

He shook his head gently, eyes never leaving mine. "Yours runs deeper. You've felt it before—sharply, painfully."

My throat tightened, an icy prickle of discomfort rippling across my skin. "What do you mean?"

He inhaled deeply, closing his eyes momentarily as if listening carefully to something beyond the room, beyond sight itself. When he reopened them, the intensity of his stare deepened, fixing me in place. "Your grandmother," he said simply. "You still carry her."

The breath caught sharply in my chest. My grandmother had passed years earlier, peacefully in her sleep, but the loss remained vivid—a wound beneath the surface, rarely discussed yet ever-present.

"How could you possibly know—"

"She's here now," he interrupted softly, with a gentleness that belied the impossibility of his claim. "She has been following you tonight."

I stared in disbelief, heart hammering violently, an aching blend of hope and incredulity rising within me. "What is this?"

He lifted one thin hand, palm upward. "Listen."

A silence fell between us, deeper and heavier than before, settling thickly around my shoulders. For a moment, nothing happened. My skepticism nearly forced a nervous laugh from my throat—then, suddenly, something shifted.

The air grew subtly warmer, carrying an aroma—faint yet unmistakable. Lavender, rich and comforting, the same scent of the soaps and lotions my grandmother always kept meticulously arranged beside her bathroom sink.

My eyes stung suddenly with tears. "What—how?"

"Shh," he whispered gently, eyes closed again, leaning toward me as though channeling something intangible yet profoundly present. His voice changed subtly, warmer now, resonant with a delicate tenderness that shook my skepticism. "You worry too much," he spoke softly, his tone slipping gradually into something hauntingly familiar. "You carry burdens you don't need."

I inhaled sharply, hands trembling atop the table. My grandmother's voice—subtle inflections, nuances of tone and rhythm, unmistakably hers—flowed through this stranger seated before me.

"You're angry," the voice continued gently, its kindness achingly familiar, each word sending chills through my body. "You've held onto your grief, thinking it honors me. But you need to let go."

My voice trembled. "Grandma?"

"Be brave, my dear boy," the voice urged gently, its sincerity achingly genuine, resonating deep in my bones. "You have love around you. Stop fearing loss and begin embracing life."

The elderly man drew a slow breath, eyes fluttering briefly before opening again, refocusing with detached, tranquil clarity. The warm lavender presence gradually receded, fading softly back into memory.

My heart pounded in stunned silence. The old man stared at me patiently, allowing space for my emotional upheaval. When he finally spoke again, his voice returned to its original quiet rasp.

"You came seeking fear, expecting it from outside yourself," he murmured, eyes solemn yet strangely compassionate. "But the greatest terror always lies within."

I nodded, unable to speak. A heavy sadness mixed with relief, cathartic yet disorienting. My heart beat unevenly, pulse echoing in my ears.

He extended one hand, grasping mine with surprising strength, his grip firm and comforting. "Go forward. Face the dark, and release what haunts you."

I rose unsteadily, legs trembling beneath me. The room spun briefly. With a final glance at the stranger—somehow both ordinary and impossible—I turned and stepped slowly toward the opposite door.

"Wait," I said quietly, pausing at the threshold, turning back hesitantly. "Who are you?"

He smiled faintly, the first genuine expression he'd revealed. "Merely another seeker who found peace," he replied cryptically. "Now I guide others." He gestured calmly toward the darkness beyond. "She's waiting for you, you know—your love. She faces her own fears, but soon enough your paths will cross again."

"Thank you," I whispered, not fully comprehending what had just transpired yet deeply grateful nonetheless.

Stepping into the corridor once again, I allowed the door to close behind me, returning to enveloping darkness. Lauren's presence drifted again into my thoughts, her laughter, her recklessness—her fierce embrace of life, fearless even in vulnerability.

I wondered briefly about her own existential encounter: what secrets might haunt her path, what ancestral voices echoed within her journey?

One thing was certain: whatever darkness lay ahead, we had chosen to face it together, even apart.

"Help wanted, inquire within," the flyer had promised.

We had asked for the unknown, the terrifying. Tonight, those words rang true beyond expectation—guiding us toward uncharted territory inside ourselves.

With renewed courage, I pressed onward, into the deepest shadows yet to come.


**Part Four: Shadows of the Mind**


Lauren stood in the encompassing darkness, breathing slowly, regaining composure after our sudden separation. The loss of touch, the absence of my warmth beside her, heightened every nerve, sharpening her awareness into razor focus.

The distant echoes of shuffling footsteps faded. She was utterly alone.

"Okay," she murmured defiantly, pushing away doubt. Her voice felt small against the pressing darkness. She straightened her dress, feeling suddenly vulnerable and undeniably exposed. Not the smartest choice, she thought ruefully, before smirking to herself. But definitely memorable.

Fingers stretched outward, Lauren navigated the dark, feeling her way along damp, rough walls that narrowed gradually, guiding her deeper into an oppressive corridor.

Suddenly, her hand brushed cold metal bars—a gate, waist high. As she climbed over it, her foot slipped on damp concrete, and she tumbled forward. Hands outstretched, she caught herself, landing heavily on all fours.

"Great," she muttered dryly, knees scraping against the rough floor. She paused, blinking in the pitch-black, feeling her way forward. Her heart quickened as she realized the corridor had narrowed sharply, the ceiling drastically lowered— forcing her onto her hands and knees.

Crawling cautiously, Lauren's breath quickened.

Claustrophobic anxiety pressed tightly against her chest. The air smelled stale, tinged with mildew and rust. Her pulse throbbed loudly in her ears.

Ahead, something shuffled softly—rhythmic, scraping steps moving closer. She froze, breath caught sharply. "Hello?"

Silence, briefly. Then a low, guttural growl—a primitive sound echoed off walls inches away.

Lauren squinted into darkness. Slowly, from shadow, a distorted silhouette emerged. A figure hunched low, moving awkwardly on all fours, blocking her path.

She gasped sharply. Its face—a grotesque mask of tangled, matted hair— obscured everything but a twisted mouth and dark, animalistic eyes. It crept closer, jerking movements insect-like, dog-like, grotesquely human.

Lauren recoiled, pulse racing, trapped in the confined space. The figure growled again, moving closer, hair-matted face inches from hers. Breath hot and rancid, a snarl of teeth flashed through knotted strands.

She suppressed panic, forcing herself steady. "Move," she demanded shakily, her voice tight yet defiant. "You're not real."
It paused, head cocked unnaturally. For a moment, it studied her, then scuttled backward, melting once again into darkness.

Lauren exhaled shakily, stunned by her own composure.
She crawled onward quickly, emerging moments later into an open room, dimly illuminated by strobing lights and flickering television screens. White noise hissed loudly from each TV, static pulsing chaotically, harsh and disorienting.

Lauren rose slowly, the cacophony assaulting her senses. Shadows danced across the walls, cast by something just beyond sight. Heart thundering, she pivoted, seeing silhouettes move fluidly, human-like yet impossibly elongated, weaving hypnotically across the flashing walls.

The flickering screens intensified, static sharpening into unbearable screeches. Lauren clamped hands over ears, stumbling forward toward a doorway silhouetted with cold blue streetlight.
Bursting outside, she gulped fresh air desperately, lungs aching, relieved at the alley's comparative normalcy. Damp asphalt gleamed beneath scattered street lamps; graffiti adorned brick walls around her.

She moved unsteadily forward, pulse gradually calming. Perhaps this was the end—an exit back to reality.

"Spare change?"

She turned sharply.

A shadowy figure emerged from behind a dumpster, shuffling closer—a homeless man, face obscured by the hood of a ragged sweatshirt.

"Sorry," she stammered, still breathless. "I don't have anything. I'm in some kind of… experience. Sorry."

The man froze, eyes narrowing suspiciously. "An experience? You think this is a joke?" His voice rose sharply, edged with aggression.

Lauren stepped backward, fear tightening her throat. "I—I didn't mean anything by—"

He lunged without warning, grabbing her wrist with surprising strength, twisting sharply. Laura cried out as he pressed her roughly against the brick wall, cold metal flashing from his pocket.

"You got money," he snarled. "Rich kids always got something. Let's see."

She trembled, panic surging sharply. The blade pressed gently against her throat—cool, threatening, terrifyingly real.

"Please," she whispered desperately, tears welling despite herself. "I swear, I don't—"

Suddenly, a violent impact struck the man from behind, knocking him sideways. Two figures materialized from shadows, tackling him roughly to the ground. Shouting voices blurred into chaos.

Lauren staggered away, heart hammering wildly, eyes wide with shock. A woman grabbed her gently by the shoulders, guiding her quickly back toward a hidden side door into the building.

"You're okay," the woman reassured firmly, her voice calming yet authoritative. "It's safe now."

Lauren exhaled heavily, legs shaking beneath her. "He… He had a knife."

"You're safe," the woman repeated soothingly, guiding Lauren through the door. "We have you."

They stepped back inside, the comforting familiarity of the dark corridors strangely reassuring. Lauren leaned against the wall, breathing ragged, eyes shut tight. Adrenaline gradually subsided, replaced by overwhelming relief.

Yet as her breathing steadied, an unsettling realization crept slowly into her consciousness. Silence filled the hallway. The woman's reassuring presence faded; she had vanished silently.

Lauren's eyes snapped open, heart sinking rapidly. The doorway she'd entered had vanished, replaced by solid concrete.

"No," she whispered, disbelievingly. Her pulse quickened again, panic tinged with grudging admiration for the sheer cleverness of the ruse.

A single, bare bulb flickered dimly, illuminating words scrawled crudely in white paint across the opposite wall:

HELP WANTED, INQUIRE WITHIN

Lauren exhaled sharply, frustration mingling with reluctant respect. They'd tricked her masterfully, blurring lines between reality and performance until both became indistinguishable. Her vulnerability had been expertly exploited, leaving her emotionally raw yet thrillingly alive.

She straightened defiantly, adjusting her dress, brushing dirt from her scraped knees. If they intended to frighten her into submission, they'd underestimated her strength. Determined and unafraid, she moved forward resolutely into the next shadowed corridor, fully embracing whatever came next.

We'd asked for an existential haunting, after all—and tonight, the darkness was delivering exactly what was promised.

**Part Five: Salt and Silk**

After my unsettling encounter with the old man, the hallway narrowed abruptly, the rough concrete walls becoming smooth plaster painted matte black. Dimly lit sconces flickered every few feet, casting sinister pools of shadow beneath my feet.

Ahead, a heavy velvet curtain parted silently, revealing a surreal and unexpected sight: a café—intimate, luxurious, draped in crimson and black velvet. Booths lined the walls, their plush red leather cushions polished under a gentle amber glow. A slow, hypnotic jazz melody seeped softly from hidden speakers, an otherworldly blend of melancholy and allure.

Cautiously, I stepped inside. The thick scent of incense, clove cigarettes, and something darker—coppery, almost metallic—hung in the air. As my eyes adjusted, I noticed silhouettes occupying the booths, murmuring quietly, indistinct shapes leaning close in intimate, shadowy conversations.

A slender figure caught my attention at once. She moved effortlessly between booths, an elegant spider gliding silkily across her web. Her raven-black hair cascaded down her back, framing porcelain-white skin marked with intricate tattoos that traced patterns both sensual and macabre. Her eyes, strikingly pale yet strangely luminous, flitted over each patron with measured intensity.

Before I could move or speak, she spotted me. Her gaze locked onto mine, and a slow, enigmatic smile curled her dark crimson lips.

"You're late," she purred softly, closing the distance swiftly. Her fingers—long, slender, adorned with silver rings—lightly traced my forearm, leaving a trail of goosebumps. "But you're here now. Come."

I felt utterly powerless, pulled by her irresistible gravity into an empty booth near the back. She eased into the seat across from me, movements fluid, deliberate, mesmerizing. Her gaze bore deeply into mine, unsettlingly intimate yet undeniably magnetic.

"You must stay," she murmured softly, eyes glittering with a hidden hunger.

I hesitated, swallowing the lump rising in my throat. "I—I can't."

A flash of displeasure crossed her features, quickly concealed behind a serene mask. Without breaking eye contact, she lifted a small silver shaker from the table. Slowly, almost reverently, she poured salt onto the polished wooden surface, forming a loose, delicate canvas.

With exquisite precision, she drew one delicate finger through the grains, tracing elegant curves and letters: STAY

I watched her hands move hypnotically, heart beating unevenly. She pushed the salt toward me, an invitation to reply. Compelled, I hesitated only briefly before tracing my finger through the grains. CAN'T

Her lips tightened slightly, eyes narrowing. With graceful insistence, she erased the word, scattering grains sharply, and carefully wrote again. FOREVER

I shook my head slowly, more firmly this time, tracing carefully through the salt: NOT POSSIBLE

Her expression darkened visibly, the warmth in her eyes turning icy, dangerous. A chill crept slowly down my spine.

"You misunderstand," she said softly, voice tinged with menace beneath seductive silk. "No isn't an option here."

I felt a surge of adrenaline, anxiety mingling with strange desire, confusion clouding my thoughts. "What… What is this place?"

She leaned forward, eyes glinting sharply. Her lips curled cruelly, revealing a glimpse of teeth just slightly sharper than seemed natural. "This is where lost things come to belong. You're already part of it."

My pulse quickened. Her magnetic pull intensified, simultaneously alluring and frightening. She reached again into the salt, drawing slowly, deliberately: MINE

My throat tightened, breath suddenly shallow, trapped by her piercing gaze. Swallowing hard, I leaned forward, writing firmly in the salt again: NO

She hissed softly, her anger flaring visibly now, barely restrained. Her delicate fingers tightened on my wrist with surprising force, nails pressing sharply into flesh.

"You asked for this," she whispered venomously, eyes burning brightly, dangerously possessive. "Help wanted, remember? You inquired within. And here you are."

She leaned closer, breath warm yet chilling against my skin, voice barely audible, seductive and threatening: "You'll stay because I demand it."

I wrenched my wrist away, panic breaking her hold. "No," I whispered defiantly, voice shaking but determined. "I won't."

For a moment, her expression faltered, disbelief giving way to furious contempt. Then suddenly, the room spun violently. Strong, unseen hands gripped my shoulders from behind, yanking me forcefully from the booth.

I stumbled backward, dragged roughly toward the door, the café dissolving around me, red leather booths fading to shadowed walls, flickering lights dimming rapidly. Her fierce eyes followed my exit, rage and betrayal etched sharply in her features.

"You'll regret this," she promised icily, her voice echoing hauntingly behind me.

Before I could reply, I was shoved violently outward, stumbling into the cold air of a familiar, dingy alleyway. Knees scraped roughly against wet asphalt. I gasped, disoriented, scrambling to my feet, heart hammering in confusion and panic.

From the shadowy corner, the same homeless figure who had confronted Lauren earlier watched me with narrowed eyes, glinting suspiciously. He took a hesitant step toward me.

"Hey, man—got any change?"

"Sorry," I said quickly, breathless, holding palms outward defensively. "I don't have anything."

He scowled, growing instantly agitated. "Just like the girl. You all think it's a joke!"

Before I could react, he lunged wildly, knife flashing dangerously in the dim streetlight. Instinctively, I raised my arms, preparing to defend myself.

A sudden shout erupted from behind me. Two powerful figures surged from the shadows, tackling my attacker roughly to the ground. The knife skittered away, harmlessly clattering against bricks.

"You okay?" asked one savior firmly, lifting me gently yet urgently.

"Yes," I stammered shakily. "Thanks—I thought—"

"Let's get you inside," he said calmly. "You're safe now."

He guided me quickly through another hidden side door. The familiar dark corridors greeted me again, unsettling yet oddly comforting after the alley's violence.

But as I regained composure, my heart sank quickly in realization. The two figures vanished silently into shadow, leaving me again alone beneath flickering lights and cryptic words painted in white:

HELP WANTED, INQUIRE WITHIN

I exhaled heavily, frustration and grudging admiration entwined. I'd been expertly manipulated, thrust again into uncertainty, the boundaries between reality and performance blurred to maddening ambiguity.

Somewhere nearby, Lauren faced her own twisted labyrinth—each step drawing us deeper into ourselves.

With newfound resolve, I moved forward, determined to reclaim control, find Lauren, and confront whatever awaited in the shadows yet to come.

**Part Six: Going Down**

I stumbled blindly through another dim corridor, disoriented, senses reeling from the relentless psychological twists. The walls pressed tighter, the air grew colder, heavier. Suddenly, rough hands grabbed me from behind. A coarse burlap sack was thrust roughly over my head, plunging me into absolute darkness.

My pulse skyrocketed as I was dragged forward. "What's going on?!" I demanded, panic edging my voice. No answer, just the steady shuffle of feet against gritty concrete. My wrists were gently bound behind me—firm, but oddly not aggressive. This felt strangely ceremonial.

Elsewhere, Lauren was navigating her own final maze. Her heart raced when unseen hands seized her as well. She gasped as the scratchy burlap enveloped her head, blocking out sight and plunging her into suffocating darkness. A rush of adrenaline surged through her veins.

Moments later, I was thrust into an enclosed space. The floor was metal and creaked underfoot—a freight elevator, I guessed from the faint smell of grease and rust. Beside me, another captive stumbled inside. We stood side by side, shoulders nearly touching, breathing unsteady. Both unaware the other was there.

A tense silence followed.

Then a low, gravelly voice broke through—deep, amused, and mocking beneath a grotesque rubber mask. "Going down?"

I hesitated, chest tight, anxiety rising. My mouth opened, but nothing came out.

Beside me, the other captive—Lauren—also hesitated. Her pulse quickened. "Yes," she said finally, voice soft but steady.

Recognition flooded through me instantly, relief and warmth surging. My heart lifted, joyfully recognizing her voice.

"Yes," I echoed, strength returning to my own voice.

Lauren inhaled sharply. "Babe?" she whispered urgently.

I turned toward her, burlap-covered face shifting awkwardly.

"Lauren! Thank God you're here."

Her shoulder pressed against mine urgently, reassuring and comforting. Even beneath restraints and burlap sacks, we leaned closer, bonded and grateful to have found each other again. With a jarring metallic clank, the elevator jolted downward abruptly. We descended steadily into the depths, the steady mechanical hum vibrating beneath our feet. The masked attendant said nothing more, fading silently into the background.

"Are you okay?" I asked quietly, urgently.

Lauren breathed deeply beside me. "Now I am," she murmured softly, voice trembling slightly. "That was intense."

"Yeah," I agreed, relief flooding my chest. "But we made it."

We stood close, silent, waiting as the elevator carried us downward—uncertain yet strangely hopeful about what awaited below. Minutes stretched endlessly, each second amplifying anticipation.

Finally, the elevator slowed to a creaking halt, coming to rest gently at the bottom level. The heavy door groaned open slowly.

Suddenly, the sacks were lifted gently from our heads. Blinding white light filled the elevator, illuminating us in pure, brilliant clarity. We blinked, squinting briefly as our vision adjusted.

The masked figure disappeared silently behind us, leaving Lauren and me standing alone. Ahead stretched a large white room, brightly illuminated, pristine walls radiating softly. In the center sat a single polished mahogany desk. Behind it stood an empty chair, perfectly centered beneath warm, comforting light.

Lauren and I embraced immediately, holding each other fiercely, savoring warmth, comfort, and relief. I brushed strands of hair from her flushed face, looking deeply into her sparkling, intense eyes.

"You're okay," I whispered softly.

She smiled, leaning closer. "We both are." She kissed me deeply, passionately, our connection reaffirmed powerfully by the ordeal we had just endured.

We stepped toward the desk cautiously, holding each other's hands firmly. On the desktop lay a single plain sheet of paper, crisp and perfect, glowing gently in the surreal illumination.

Before we could say anything, a soft, disembodied voice echoed warmly through unseen speakers, gentle yet commanding:

"Congratulations. You have completed your existential journey."

Lauren and I exchanged cautious smiles, hearts still beating rapidly with exhilaration and residual anxiety. The voice continued smoothly, calmly:

"You've seen yourselves and each other at your most vulnerable. You have faced isolation, temptation, terror, and truth."

We nodded slowly, deeply moved yet unsure what came next. Lauren squeezed my hand tightly.

"You have inquired within," the voice said, warmth in its tone increasing gently. "You asked for help, and you have found something profound within yourselves."

We waited breathlessly, fingers intwined, shoulders pressed gently together.

The voice paused meaningfully, then spoke again, calmly, deliberately: "So...are you interested in the job?"

We looked at each other instantly, startled, amused, confused. Then, slowly, realization dawned—understanding this experience had been not just a haunting but a bizarre, beautifully twisted initiation. We'd been tested, measured, challenged, and judged worthy.

I laughed softly, shaking my head in amazement. Lauren smiled brilliantly, eyes sparkling. She leaned into me, her lips brushing my ear, whispering gently, "Do you think they're serious?"

I smiled back warmly, sensing clearly the absurd yet irresistible invitation. "I think they are."

We turned again toward the glowing desk, grinning despite our confusion and exhaustion. After the madness of tonight, reality felt pliable, negotiable.

"Maybe we should inquire further," Lauren teased playfully, nudging me gently.

"It is why we came." I chuckled, nodding decisively. "Together?"

"Always," she whispered firmly.

Hand-in-hand, we stepped forward, ready to accept whatever enigmatic, thrilling opportunity awaited us next. Our fears, our passions, our weaknesses—all revealed and confronted tonight—now strengthened our bond, opening a tantalizing door to possibilities we'd never imagined.

Tonight had not been an ending at all—but a strange, beautiful beginning.

The soft voice spoke once more, reassuring, expectant: "Well then...welcome aboard."

A hidden door slid silently open behind the desk, revealing a new path—brightly lit, mysterious, beckoning us forward.

Lauren squeezed my hand again, exhilarated, unafraid, daring me onward with mischievous eyes.

We stepped through together, hearts beating fast, fully prepared now to embrace the unknown awaiting us ahead.

# Space Pasture Blues

by B.W.Hunt

Callum blinks awake to the sound of a strange alarm. It's distant, but loud enough to drag him from sleep. He shifts against the straps holding him to his bunk, and squints around the cramped sleeping module. The room groans, followed by a loud click and the hiss of air pressure shifting a few chambers away. The docking alarm begins to whir, sounding closer to Cal and less aggressive than the one that woke him.

He unfastens his restraints and lets himself drift to the port window. Anansi Station hangs at a harsh angle against an inky black backdrop, littered with stars. From where he hovers, he can make out a vast, curved window wrapping around a stark, white central terminal. Many smaller modules fan out from the terminal like a web, connected with small, windowed passages for the crew to maneuver. Inside one of these modules, Cal spots a plot of lush green grass, and a few indistinct shapes that he determines to be his new goats.

He looks closer and smiles, speaking aloud as he often does, "Must be about twenty of 'em. Should be easy enough." Then he turned to continue his preparations, but an odd feeling struck him, and he stopped abruptly. "Surely I must be mad." He mutters and twists his head back to the window. "A goat..."

Indeed, there is a goat, perhaps fifty feet from his port window, drifting along in the space between his shuttle and the station. Its space helmet gleams against the unburdened sun, and he could swear it's looking right at him. As it drifted casually through the darkness, its tail wiggled with excitement. He spots three workers in spacesuits. not far behind the adventurous goat, holding a tether and communicating quietly as they slowly gained on the creature. They look over at Cal, smile, and wave in a sarcastic gesture of welcoming. His door opens with a hiss, and he takes in the ridiculous scene for one more moment before turning to board. He ponders to himself as he walks, "That must be the *troubled goat* they warned me about".

It was quite a strange job. A farmer on Anansi Station had a family emergency in the Big City on Mars and needed someone to look after his goats until he could return. Callum never did well with crowds, but he likes goats, and Anansi seems like a quiet place to return to his routine. A month or so prior to setting a course for Anansi, Cal had lost his family farm, when a rogue booster from a local shuttle careened into his barn, igniting everything in an oily flame.

It seemed to Cal that he was at the end of his rope, wandering through his hometown, deciding how he could possibly rebuild and proceed with his career, when he spotted a sign at the end of a damp alley. "Help Wanted, Inquire Within" It read in bold, streaky lettering on an oxidized piece of white metal. It looked as if it was done in a hurry. Cal hesitated outside the door for a few moments before deciding he had no other option but to do as the sign instructed. He entered the door, letting it close behind him with a wooden creak. He was put on a shuttle off-planet and told to meet a man named Jack before he could even take in his surroundings. He was a space herder now.

A ragged man in a straw hat waits by the entrance to Anansi at the end of the hall connecting the two vessels. He nurses a tobacco pipe, making thick plumes of smoke rise from the embers. He looks up, still puffing, and watches Callum approach from a distance. When Cal finally reaches the man, they stand a few feet apart in silence as the man examines him from top to bottom.

"I don't think you should be smoking that in here" Cal says hesitantly, "Limited oxygen and all."

The man grins wider, the tip of the pipe still clenched between his teeth. Without a word, he flicks a used matchstick at Cal, hitting him square in the forehead. It tumbles to the floor without a sound.

"My lord!" Cal spits out, "Are you well?"

The man groans, and his grin fades. He reaches out a hand, "I'm Jack."

"A pleasure, I suppose." Cal shakes his hand hesitantly.

"You good with goats, kid?" Jack asks, taking another deep drag from the pipe, reigniting the wooden bowl and letting it billow out rings of smoke. He watches them rise.

Cal found himself watching the smoke as well, reminding him of simpler times and life on a giant rock. He says, "Pretty good. Not as good as some but better than most."

Jack nods, hitting the large orange button that opens the bulkhead into the greater portions of Anansi Station. He walks in, eyes never wavering from the path ahead. Cal follows, keeping up with Jack's steady pace.

As they approach the steel double-door that presumably leads to the pasture, Jack speaks, "Daisy." He waits to see if he has Cal's attention. He does, so he continues. "Daisy is... a different sort of goat, she'll be most of your work, I'm sure." He takes another puff.

"Is she the one I saw joyriding in space a moment ago?" Cal asks with a smile.

Jack laughs hardily for a moment longer than Cal would've expected, catches his breath and then speaks again, "Look, kid, the staff here is going to take me off station a few thousand miles to the shuttle station, so you'll be on your own tonight. Can you keep her indoors?"

"I'll keep a closer eye on her than God himself, Jack." He waits for a reaction but got none. "I'm good for it," He adds sheepishly

"I hope so." Jack says, more solemn than before. He then reached an arm out to his side to push the button that opens the doors. They shift with a similar hiss and Cal feels a gentle heat emanating from the opening. A green hue pours onto the white walls around them. As they entered, they were greeted by the curious eyes of about twenty goats, hidden behind the glare of their space helmets.

"Why do they wear those?" Callum asks, confused, as he had never seen space equipment designed for animals. Goats are the most common low-gravity livestock, as they handle the lacking gravitational forces better than the rest. Cows tend to tip, and chickens can't help but flap when they lifted from a surface, disorienting them and throwing them further from their intended destination. He had herded many goats in his time on Earth, a dingey farm planet with not much in the way of entertainment, and he figured this would be good, honest work.

"This pasture's a special case, buddy." Jack says flatly.

"What makes it such a special case?" Cal asks.

"We have a..." Jack hesitates, "containment issue." He chuckles to himself and continues onward.

"Daisy, you mean?" Cal asks again, "Why not just get rid of her?"

Jack pauses his movement, not looking back, and after a second or two of deep thought, he says, "I kind of like her."

Jack spends the next couple of hours showing Cal where all the goats' amenities are located, where to fetch feed and clean water, and where to pen them when he goes to sleep. Cal listens intently, but Jack has the sense he didn't need to be so thorough. He can see that Cal is an experienced goatherd. He maintains his unimpressed composure. After some time, Jack gives his final goodbyes and callous thanks to Cal before heading out to his shuttle pod, followed by the three other staff members aboard Anansi. They give Cal the same sarcastic waves they'd given him from outside the shuttle window, and Cal begins to realize he may be in for an irregular night.

Alone at last, and after tending to the herds' basic needs, Cal settles into a wooden chair at the corner of the pasture, placed to keep a casual eye on the goats while he rests. He takes a book from his pack and places it on the side table next to him. He monitors the goats carefully, taking stock of his responsibility for the next month or so. He counts them, twenty-four in total as Jack stated before his departure.

"Twenty-one... Twenty-two..." he counts aloud, feeling an incredible relief at the simplicity and routine of his new daily tasks, "Twenty-three... and..." He stops.

Twenty-four is nowhere in sight. He stands, and paces into the herd. They shuffle around him, helmets bobbing and suits jingling as they do so, bleating obliviously. He counts them once more, and to his dismay, he is halted again at twenty-three. He rubs his temples anxiously. The "containment leak" must have gotten loose again. He knows his only choice was to pen the goats and start his search. He rounds them up with a masterful call and paces quickly toward the supply closet. There he finds a flashlight, which he brings back into the pasture and begins to inspect the ducts along the floor and ceiling. None of them seem out of place; they're all closed tight. He begins to panic.

"Oh lord, Oh Jesus. Jack won't like this one bit." He desperately pleads with his brain to come up with some kind of idea. His hands pull at his hair in dire stress, and he turns toward the window. "Daisy!" He yelped with both excitement and terror.

Beyond the window, amongst the cosmic tide, without a care in the world, Daisy floats. Her tail wiggles and her legs kick in a swimming motion, ineffective against the vacuum of space. She looks straight at Cal, and he springs into action. He heads toward the departure room with fearful haste. The bulkhead leading inside is heavier than expected, and Cal exhausts himself trying to force it open. Once inside, he fumbles the space suit off of its hook and starts to shove his leg in through the back zipper.

"What the hell am I doing?!" Cal asks himself. "I can't go out there... I'm not trained... I..." His dread momentarily takes full control, when he spots Daisy through the airlock window, barely a dot in the sea of black, "Shit."

He suits up shakily, and with slow and tentative steps, he makes his way into the airlock, closing the door behind him. "Oh God. Oh God, please." Cal speaks to nobody as he lets his hand linger on the control to open the outer door. He closes his eyes, and after several moments, he pulls the lever.

Space is silent within the suit, and the station seems to make no sound at all as a chasm between safety and death opens before him. Cal slowly pulls himself to the opening, and straps himself to a thick orange tether line, "rated for twenty miles" printed along the mechanism. He notices then that another tether line was already set loose, its end disappearing into space in Daisy's direction. He ignores this, and taking one last, deep breath, he propels himself into space, toward Daisy, toward his doom.

He drifts seemingly forever, and the dot began to grow into the bare shape of an animal. Her space helmet gives off a reflective beacon for Cal to follow. He wants to maintain a similar speed to Daisy, as he doesn't want to accidentally run into her at a hundred feet per second. The monopropellant jetpack he uses to control his speed is very sensitive, and every adjustment needs to be done with extreme caution.

"Good lord." Cal says as he looks back toward Anansi, now also a dot on the metaphorical horizon. Daisy was close now, and Cal can make out the devious look in her eyes. She knows she's been caught, and the fun is over. He wraps his arms around her gently, and he thumbs the control for the airlock mechanism to begin retrieving the tether. "I got you now, girl." Daisy bleats cheerfully, loud enough to be heard through both helmets.

Cal guesses they both made it about eleven miles before they reached each other, and the screen on the wrist of his spacesuit proves him almost right. It reads "13.1 mi" in a basic rounded font. Cal sighed, "I can't believe you, Daisy. This is the last place in the universe I want to be, and yet here I am." He says this in an endearing and playfully upset tone. He is just glad it's nearly over.

He feels a hard pull on his left hip, and begins to spin, picking up speed. "Woah!" he grunts, latching his arms onto Daisy with everything he has, "Hang on girl!" He yells, feeling his grip slipping briefly but finding purchase on a strap attached to Daisy's suit. Their spin quickly becomes violent, and the tether begins to whip around in uncontrollable circles. He is blinded by dizziness and painfully aware of his ever-faltering grip on the goat. The bright stars become streaks in his vision as they continue their disorienting ballet. Cal realizes one of his thrusters is jammed on. The hand he needs to free himself is holding fast to the goat's strap, and the other simply won't reach.

Clenching his teeth, and holding on with everything he has left, he speaks to Daisy, "I gotta let go, girl." Tears cover his eyes, "I'm so sorry. I'm so, so sorry, Daisy." He continues to hold on. His vision begins to fade. The spinning becomes too much for him, and his head swims in and out of consciousness. He pulls his arms as tightly around Daisy as they will go before succumbing to the fog overtaking his mind. The last thing he hears is the sound of Daisy responding with a loud bleat, before his world vanishes into blackness.

...

Cal blinks awake to another loud bleating directly in his ear, more frantic than the ones he'd become accustomed to. He's on the ground, he realizes, solid ground. White LED strips light the space around him from above. His head throbs rhythmically. He leans his head to inspect the rest of his body, somehow still alive. Wrapped tightly in his arms is Daisy, who looked annoyed. Cal laughed exhaustedly and released his grip.

"Lucky girl. Guess I couldn't do it." He says to the moody goat, who gratefully removed herself from Cal's grasp and shook off her stiff muscles. Cal could barely stand, but he dragged himself up to the airlock door and opened it to let Daisy back inside. He went to follow, but the tether was still hooked to the front of his belt. He unlatches it, clips his end to her strap and steps up through the bulkhead.

Callum sets the spacesuit down against the wall just outside of the airlock. Completely devoid of energy, he slumps onto the floor next to it and sighs. Daisy bleats to his right, her helmet bumping against Cal's as she stumbles by him obliviously, back into the greater station. He watched her wander a small distance away as he removed the helmet from his aching neck, holding the tether so she couldn't go far. He sat there for a long time, considering the gravity of the situation he had found himself in just moments ago. A part of him wants to cry, but instead he chuckles to himself.

"My lord." he says aloud, "The things I do for you damn animals."

Daisy tugs on the length of the tether for a moment before giving in to her confinement and laying on the floor, a few feet away from Cal. She bleats quietly.

"You must be exhausted too, huh?" He looks inquisitively at the goat, "I think we've both had enough of your hijinks for a day or two, wouldn't you say?" He cranes his head toward the airlock door and notices a small leather satchel on a hook just next to it. He hadn't noticed it when he left, and as it was within arm's reach, he pulls it off the hook lazily and opens it on his lap. A pipe, and a small store of tobacco held in a wooden box, the lid needing to be slid off from the top. Cal had never smoked, but boy did it smell good! He pulls the pipe out, stuffs it full, lights a match and inhales it deeply through the curved mouthpiece.

"By God, Jack!" he says as the smoke trails in whisps from his mouth, "I think I like her too." Cal remembered the second tether, broken and drifting beside the station, and figured Jack must have left this pouch here in case of a similar circumstance.

He considers the job application in his mind as he smokes, leaning comfortably against the smooth walls and feeling content. 'Troubled Livestock', an understatement if there ever was one. He chuckles again and looks over at the rambunctious goat as she drifted off to sleep.

He said to her, cheerfully and defeated, "What on Earth are we gonna do with you, Daisy? We both know this won't be the last time, don't we?"

Daisy bleats in response, almost inaudibly. Cal smiles, the pipe clenched between his teeth.

"I guess that's just..." He takes one more long drag from the pipe, slumping down further to lay flat on the cold, steel floor. He chuckles again, exhausted, thinking about the first time he saw Daisy. "Never mind..."

Cal falls asleep, content and reassured, cozy and alive, snug and warm in the artificial gravity, and as he does so, the tether falls from his hands.

# Feelings
## by Kyle N. Kolber

"Help wanted, Inquire within."

Hell, that's what the sign said, that stupid little sign taped on that old beaten door in that random alleyway in Los Angeles.

I would've loved to know what the purpose of that sign was, and heck, I still don't. It doesn't make sense what that "job" was that paid a thousand dollars; I needed the money.

Being an actor in this world full of Ryan Goslings and Mark Ruffilos just wasn't fair. I applied for every role that came my way, auditioned, and hoped to get it. Once I got the "no" and learned what other big star had achieved my dream, I moved on to the next one. This happened over and over again, for the last three years I've been in this godforsaken city, three whole years, one thousand and ninety-five days.

I was waiting tables—I know, the usual gig for actors—when one of my coworkers pulled me aside from the back. Her short brown hair and green eyes pierced mine as she told me about a gig she heard about, not a gig to act, but one to make a quick grand. Her friend of a friend did it, and now she told me about it, thinking I could use the help. She was right, I could. She wrote down the address and said, and I remember this part distinctively, "It's outside it. Not inside. Like outside it. You'll know what I mean."

I didn't.

The next day I went to the address, which led me to a small coffee shop with bright colors and groups of young people in windows—probably having first dates or about to break up. I started to walk into the shop when a voice in my head that wasn't mine, but a deep scuff of a voice so long and dead, spoke, "You know not to go in there, Phillip. I'm not in there."

I looked to my left, then my right, seeing no one around me. I looked into the windows of the coffee shop, still seeing the people eating away with whoever they were with. In the air, I heard the city sounds of cars beeping and people chattering…then the sound of music. It wasn't a song I knew, or one I think was ever created, but a sound that buzzed in my mind to find where it was coming from. There was an orchestra, playing faintly and slowly, eliminating the sounds of the city around me- slowly but surely getting louder. I heard the violin, the trumpets, the drums, playing and singing in my ears. It pulled me. My feet moved to the side of the coffee shop, going in between two buildings down an alleyway, and that's where I saw it, *the door*.

At the end of the alleyway, etched into the brick wall, was the beaten door with a taped paper sign with words written in Sharpie, "HELP WANTED, IN-QUIRE WITHIN."

The music from the inside strung in a muffled tone and shouted from within, and with each step I took, grew more and more dramatic, the strings shouting. When I reached the door, I slowly reached down to the black doorknob. The music shouted in anticipation in a long high note, I turned the knob, opened the door, and the music stopped.

Inside was a gray room with one bright light fixture on the ceiling, and a perfect concrete tile floor. In the center of the room was a woman sitting behind a desk, with a typewriter, clicking away at whatever she was typing. She was younger, had a messy bun with glasses, and was in a suit. When I walked in, she didn't even look up from her typewriter, she just kept typing, clicking and clacking away.

Behind the woman was a white door going to God knew where. I took a few steps in, hearing the door behind me close. There was nothing else in the room, just her and I, and that damn typewriter, clicking…clicking…clicking.

I asked, "Excuse me? Where am I?"

The woman stopped and looked up from her work, eyeing me up all around, then looked back down at her typewriter, typing. She announced, "We've been expecting you, Phillip."

I titled my head, "We?"

She didn't look up, "Yes, me and the man. *We.*"

A feeling of anxious tension hit my stomach- feeling like something wasn't right, so I turned around to leave, and I saw nothing but a wall. There was no door- just a gray wall. I then turned around again, eyes widened, heart pumping, "Where is-"

But I was cut off by the woman, "The door is gone. You're here now. Do you want you're thousand dollars or not?"

I took an easy deep breath, trying to calm myself down…trying to at least. A thousand dollars would've gone a long way- a very long way, and I didn't seem to have a way out. I took a deep breath and answered, "I do want the money."

The woman continued typing, "Good, now go in."

And as she said that, the door behind her opened. Alert and ready I walked past her and took a glance at the piece of paper she was typing on, it was completely blank.

Inside the door was the same kind of room with a single desk in the middle, except this time it was an old Black man with gray hair, a long smile, and white eyes sitting at it. He was sitting at a computer, and on the other side of the desk was a different computer facing away from him. The computers were old. They resembled those old, box-like computers from the early 2000s. The kind of computers that could run just a few internet features like solitaire and chess, but nothing else. There was no other door inside this room, nowhere in sight. The man faced forward with a long smile, not looking at me but looking past me. He had his hands on the desk and was breathing very slowly- much too slowly. The man announced in a sing-song voice, "Don't mind the eyes, I'm just blind."

That didn't help anything. I continued to stand still and stare at this man. He reached over to the computers, and slowly pushed them to the side, gesturing to the chair in front of him. He sang, "Please, Phillip, sit."

And so I did. I felt like I had to. I eased my way into the chair, staring at the blind Black man, as he seemingly stared right back. I waved my hand at his face, seeing if he was *really* blind. He didn't move, he just continued to stare with that smile etched across his face. He was blind. I asked, "What do you want with me?"

He had a long hard laugh, "Well Phillip, we *want* your feelings."

"My feelings?"

"Yes. We want to see how you feel about certain colors."

Confused as can be, I asked, "What are you talking about?"

The man leaned in, and when he spoke I smelt the stench of rot. It was as if inside him there was rot so deep and gone, that it decayed and killed just a little more with each word he spoke, "Well Phillip, here in our little corporation, we want to know how people feel about certain things. We just need you to look at a few colors, see what they make you feel, and put them in the right category."

I asked, "What kind of experiment is this?"

The man shook his head, "If *you* want it to be an experiment it can be, but it really isn't. We just *need* your feelings."

I leaned back a little, trying to get away from the smell of his breath, "and if I give you my opinion, I'll get a thousand dollars?"

He shook his head, "It's not your opinion, it's *your feelings.*"

"Right. My feelings."

The man nodded his head, "Then yes, you'll get your money," then he pointed to his left, I followed his finger and saw a door that wasn't there before, "But if you want to leave, do so now."

I looked at the door, then back at the man. At the time I just thought he needed some kind of statistic, some sort of details for science that I was getting paid for- that was at the time. I shook my head, "No, I'll stay."

The man smiled a little more, "Good."

I looked over to the door, it was gone.

The old man had slid the computer back in front of me. Having a closer look, the computer looked so old that I may have been a few years younger than it. There was a hum rising from the insides as if it was running on its last legs, running and running as fast as it could go. On the screen was a black background with two words in lime green boxes, "good and bad". And in the middle was my mouse cursor. I picked up the mouse and jiggled it around, seeing it lag a little as I moved it. The man spoke, "Now, the task is simple. You'll see a color, and you'll either press good or bad."

I nodded, "Sounds easy enough."

And so it happened. The screen flashed white. It wasn't just a vanilla kind of white, it was a bright white. The kind of white that you see when you're looking at your phone in the pitch-black darkness, the blinding kind. I looked at the color for the two seconds it was there, felt really no harsh feeling towards it, and then pressed "good."

A second later, a second color flashed on my screen. This time black. It wasn't like a black shirt or pants, just *black.* It made me uncomfortable- like something was watching me from inside the screen. My instinct went to "bad", so I pressed it. The man behind my computer laughed, "Someone's seen Star Wars. Don't like Darth Vader?"

I ignored him. The next color was a hot pink. It flashed, then stung my eyes, making me squint. And right then, right when that color hit, I felt something. It wasn't a good or bad feeling, it was a sucking feeling. Like something in me was being sucked out. My first reaction was going to go for the "bad," but something in me told me to press "good," that for some reason this was a *good* feeling. So, I clicked it.

A new color flashed, orange, and once again, that feeling of sucking came to me. My brain started to fuzz and my body felt a little weaker. I moved the cursor to "bad," and pressed it. My brain swung a little and my body ached, somehow, I felt weaker…much weaker. But I kept my mind going or attempted to.

The next color was purple, and my mind fuzzed- going dark, I know how that sounds, but that's the best way to describe it. The world around me spun which made my head swing back and forth…back and forth…back and-

The old man spoke, "Are you okay, Phillip?"

I muttered, "Yeah."

And pressed "bad."

The final color came…but it wasn't just one color. It was a flurry of different ones. Different colors sped up and fired in my direction…red…green….blue…

red....yellow...I couldn't press "good" or "bad," I didn't have time. The colors flashed and flashed, coming at me at high speeds, flashing and flashing, my head spinning and spinning, the sound around me cutting in and out like a person turning a speaker off and on. They kept coming, yellow...pink...yellow...my head spun more. The man asked, "Philliiipppppppp, areee you okayyyy?"

I didn't answer. He asked again with a laugh, "Phillipppppppp?"

And that's when it went black. I couldn't see anything, feel anything, be anything. Everything and anything went away...and soon I fell unconscious.

The beeping of a heart monitor woke me up, and I found myself in a hospital bed. I learned that two days prior I was found on the side of a road unconscious. No one knew what happened—they couldn't find a drug in my system or a physical injury. Next to me on a chair were my clothes along with an envelope labeled, "For Phillip."

I looked at the envelope and I knew what it was.

*The cash.*

Whatever that man put me through, he ended up paying for. For the next twenty-four hours, I stayed in that hospital bed while they monitored me. The beeping and clicking of the hospital didn't bring me any uncomfortableness or annoyance, I was just neutral. Nothing in that hospital actually alarmed me as hospitals usually did.

When I was discharged I left with the envelope in hand, not opening it, walking through the city to my small shitty apartment. Going through the city I walked past homeless people asking for money- not feeling any sympathy for them. I was shoulder-checked by a bigger man- I wasn't annoyed by him. I even saw a couple holding hands that usually would've made me gag in my mouth- to find nothing in me.

When I got to my place I sat on my couch, opened a beer, and put on "The Middle," to decompress. Usually, the comedy show would make me laugh wildly, but at every punchline, there was no laugh from me, just a stare. I stared as the TV moved, its different colors not affecting me. I just watched- stale...stale...stale.

Lying in bed that night, when I usually overthought about my life and its choices, I felt nothing. I just stared at the ceiling, watching it stay black all night long, not moving...not moving...not reacting- save only the lights of passing cars. The ceiling was dull, as were my insides, they felt dull...gone...stale.

The next day I decided to go back to that coffee shop with the envelope in my pocket. When I got there it was the same place full of bright colors, but this time there was no music in the air, nothing luring me to the door I saw the other day. Instead of trying to go into the store like I did before, I went back down the alleyway...to see nothing but a brick wall. No door, no sign, no nothing, just a wall, a wall that looked at me with a smile so large and so insidious- a smile I couldn't look at. I didn't feel anything in me though- except the need to look inside the envelope. And when I did I saw the thousand dollars in hundreds, crisp and real. And with the cash was a little piece of paper with writing on it:

"Thanks for your feelings, have a good life."

I looked at the paper for a few long seconds and felt nothing, no feelings... no nothing, just emptiness. Then I made the trudge back to my apartment.

Over the next few weeks, I tried to make myself feel normal. I watched "La La Land", a film that usually forced a tear out of me—I felt nothing. I went to comedy clubs to hear aspiring comedians tell jokes on stage. While everyone else laughed, I sat in complete silence and without emotion.

The days became longer, the nights more meaningless, and each breath felt like I was losing a little more of myself. When at work I had to force a smile and mask the hole I felt in my chest. My coworker asked me how the gig was, "So how was it? Did you get the money?"

She looked into my eyes with those piercing green ones that looked so happy and full of life. I answered her with a fake smile, "It went well."

I went back to waiting tables.

About a month later, late at night, I received an email from a casting director about a role I landed. The director of this coming-of-age film, about a boy and a girl falling in love, found my audition tapes so authentic—they couldn't pass me up. I stared at this email with the same face I'd been wearing for the past weeks, long and dead. At the end of the email, there was a sentence that would've made the old me jump for joy, *"We're going to make you a star."*

I watched that last line for a long time. I thought about how people always said that being successful could lead to a feeling of emptiness, that being a famous star with all this money could cause so many problems. Then I wondered if what I was feeling was the same for every celebrity. Maybe it was *just* me…or maybe it's what all stars felt- the cost of getting fame was losing all real feeling.

I closed my computer with a sigh, went to my apartment window, and stared up at the dark sky- seeing the stars twinkle and burn far off in the universe. Watching those stars from my apartment on that night- a night that changed my life forever, I wondered if something was watching me, choosing my life for me, and paving a path for me to go on. Then I wondered if that path was meant to have those colors that sucked my life out.

# No Experience Necessary

## Necessary
by Jeremy Miller

Be careful what you wish for.

I should have learned that from Wishmaster. Or Wishmaster 2: Evil Never Dies. Or Wishmaster 3: Beyond the Gates of Hell. Or possibly even from Wishmaster 4: The Prophecy Fulfilled.

Or a million other movies and TV shows and books and short stories and parables and homilies and folk tales. Monkey's paws and so forth. There was even an episode of the X-Files about it.

Quitting my job didn't even feel good. I thought it would feel great, at least in the moment. Take this job and shove it! And I didn't even get a period of "I'm free!" euphoria. Not even a second. I was already stressing about money while I was quitting.

No one cared. Everyone hates their job. I learned that from Office Space. Or 9 to 5. Or the Devil Wears Prada. Or Horrible Bosses. Or from real life where everyone complains about their job all the live long day.

You hate but you don't quit. You just go and keep going and wait to die. That's life.

Quitting your job is like angrily hurling a rock at the sun because you got a sunburn. Especially if you throw that rock straight up and it comes back down to hit you in the eyeball. The good eye. Righty.

I did quit.

So why did I do it? Evidently, I'm a moron.

Well, what's done is done. Get another job and move on. People get jobs all the time, right? How hard can it be? Pretty hard actually. What I've learned is, the only jobs that exist now are sales. And sales management. And nursing. I can only assume that what's being sold is nursing care.

Every movie from the '80s tried to warn me: American jobs were going away. But I didn't listen. I'm sorry, Micheal Keaton, I should have listened! In my defense, I was a decade away from actually getting a job when I watched those movies so the message was never going to get through.

There's also OnlyFans. I see stories online constantly about how women are all quitting their jobs as brain surgeons and rocket scientists because they can make more money on OnlyFans. Are there that many nursing care sales jobs to support all those women on OnlyFans? What's the breaking point? How many women can be on OnlyFans before the entire system collapses? Did any financial experts see OnlyFans as the death sentence of the global economy? Probably.

Creating and posting scam job listings online seems to be a rising segment of the job market too. Or maybe AI does that. Nobody talks about all the scammers put out of business by technology. Poor bastards. After reading my 99 millionth fake job posting, I started to think that maybe scamming people is the career path of the future.

But then we run into what I've coined as The OnlyFans Conundrum. We can't all be scammers right? Someone has to have the money to scam. If everyone is a scammer, where does the money come from? Where does money come from anyway? How does the economy even work? The entire concept of wealth collapses under you like a folding chair at an indy wrestling show if you think about it too much. I've lost weight since that show. That was a wake-up call.

"Help Wanted Inquire Within" read the sign on the door at the end of the creepy Silent Hill alleyway lit by a bare bulb shedding just enough light to artfully frame a bloody murder victim. Well sure, why not? Anyone who can't find a job isn't looking hard enough right? I mean what kind of human being doesn't have a job? That's like a bear that doesn't like salmon. It's an abomination before God. Possibly even before God.

Why was I down in the liminal horror alley to see the sign in the first place? I'd like to say I don't remember how I got there because that would be cool and creepypasta-ish but I do remember. I was walking around and I just went down there on a lark. Possibly on a whim.

What else did I have to do? There's only so many hours (or being honest, a time better measured in minutes) you can google "remote IT jobs" day after day. What else do you have to do to fill your days as an unemployed worthless piece of human garbage? There's only so many Tubi original movies you can consume before even going outside, into the world, and walking seems like a good idea.

Walking is better than my two other primary unemployed hobbies - staring at the wall or lying flat on the floor face down. Walking is better because it doesn't take much concentration, but it takes some. Walking occupies enough of your attention to keep you from turning over in your mind for the 100,000$^{th}$ time how every career decision you made in your life was wrong.

Why did I go to school for accounting? Why did I work in mortgages for 20 years? Why did I decide I wanted a change and get into IT? Why did I quit my IT job with zero plan for what comes next? Why didn't I work harder on that biology project in 9$^{th}$ grade? That's where it all started going wrong. B+? What kind of life can someone expect to have when they can't ace freshman biology?

I didn't actually expect the door to open. Even though it had a sign inviting people in to inquire within, it seemed like the kind of door that wouldn't open. Some doors just have that "won't open" air about them you know? Which has to be frustrating for the door since its entire purpose in the world is to be opened. Otherwise, it would be a wall. I wonder if there are any jobs out there for being a wall. Seems like something I could do reasonably well.

The door did open though. It opened just fine. Good job, door. You did it!

Behind the green door I expected to find a Needful Things style curio shop with some Hammer Films Peter Cushing/Christopher Lee type standing there in funky out-of-date clothes steepling their hands, pretending not to be the devil.

As per usual I was wrong.

The room beyond the door didn't look like a business of any kind. What it looked like more than anything was the build room at my old job. If you've never worked in IT; first of all congratulations, you made better life choices than me; and second of all a build room is where you keep dozens of tubs of cords and old hard drives waiting to be wiped (sanitized if you're fancy) and laptops that have been imaged but then everyone forgot about them and someone is working off their personal laptop even though that's in violation of company policy because the ticket went in the wrong queue and then in stand-up that day the database admins were pissed because the change the night before . . .

Sorry, never mind all that. Okay, it's like this, you probably have an uncle who was "into computers" in the '80s right? It looked like his spare bedroom where he keeps all his "projects". Only with a counter. So that part anyway was kind of like a business. There was a counter bisecting the room like it was a sub sandwich shop. Which it was not. There was no tuna scoop. I checked.

Behind and on the counter was a fellow in a classic counter worker's lean – groin pressed right up on their side and bent as far forward as possible. In this case the bend was to facilitate reading a book. The cover of the book had a mask on it, not like a Halloween mask but like a mask a lady in a ballgown would wear in some drama where rich people are rich in olden times and they're having a party. Maybe in England. *Cincuenta sombras más oscuras* was the title.

What about the fellow? He was neither short nor fat but he was both shorter and fatter than me, which was nice. It was a little morale boost. I may not have a job but I'm slightly more attractive than you, bub! On the other hand, he was younger and his beard was free of gray. So maybe it was a draw in the looks battle. He was a Kevin Smith, Jon Gabrus, Nick Mundy, all put into a blender and mixed together type. He looked like he should have been wearing a backwards ballcap but he wasn't. You know the kind of guy I mean.

He didn't look up from his book when I came in, which is rude, but he did look up when I asked, "What are you reading?"

I immediately regretted my question. I used to read on my lunch break and it annoyed me when people would come up and ask, "What are you reading?" Because I was trying to read, you see, not have a stupid conversation. And, and, AND, no matter what I said 100% of the time the response would be "never heard of it". Of course you haven't heard of it, Warren! Why would you have?! If you read anything since high school you would know that people who are reading on their lunch break don't like to be interrupted with your inane bullshit! Eat your cup of noodles and shut up, you worm!

Ahem, anyway, I didn't feel too bad about it though because of the sign. The sign said to come in and inquire. And asking what someone is reading is literally an inquiry.

He turned the book for a moment to look at the cover "I think it's Fifty Shades of Gray."

"Isn't gray 'gris' in Spanish?"

"I don't know" he said, setting the book aside without bothering to mark his page.

"You don't speak Spanish?"

"No" he shook his head, "it's slow going" he admitted, anticipating my next question.

I vaguely head-jerked towards the door behind me "I saw your sign."

"Cool" he said, settling into a hand-clasp with his forearms on the counter.

"Uh, I'm inquiring."

He nodded and then shook his head slightly like he was surprised "Oh right. Sorry, uh, sorry, yeah, it's been a while since anyone came in here. So yeah, basically the deal is this, uh, place is cursed. If you agree to take my place then you'll be trapped here and I get to be free."

I laughed a single conversational non-indicative of humor 'HA' to acknowledge his lame joke. "Yeah, I know what you mean, work does feel like a curse sometimes. Is this a place where you dispose of old printers and equipment? E-cycling?"

"No" he straightened up for a moment and looked around "well, maybe it was, I don't know. Like for real, this is a cursed, uh, room. I know you won't believe me but that's the deal. If you agree to stay here then I'm not trapped here anymore, and you will be until you get someone else to switch with you."

I leaned against the counter myself, with the hip though, like a gentleman. "So is this for TikTok? You clown some doofuses and then post it online for people to laugh at? Because I'll be your patsy if there's any money for doing it."

"No" he said, picking the book back up and opening to a random page, "no one ever believes me but that's what it is."

"If that was true why would anyone agree to be trapped here?"

His only response was a shrug.

"How did you get here?"

He put the book back down with a non-verbal sigh "The guy here before tricked me into agreeing to take his place. Not that it was much of a trick. He asked me in German I think and I could tell by his uh, inflection or rhythm or whatever that he was asking me a question, so I just nodded because I didn't know what he was saying. Then he got really happy and left and I've been trapped here since then. Once I figured out what he did, I told myself that I wouldn't do the same thing, I'd tell the truth and if someone wants to take my place fine, if not that's fine too."

"Okay, and how did the German guy get here?"

"I don't know" he said tiredly "and I don't know what this place is or how it happened either, I just know that for me to leave someone else has to take my place."

"You're not going to get very far on nosleep with that story, you can't have that much ambiguity, you need more background than that. That's thin even by reddit standards."

A flash of irritation came over his face before returning to Smith-Gabrus-Mundy zen. "How would I figure out what's going on here? I'm just here."

"Okay, let's say, as a thought experiment, that I believe you. What would you say to convince me to swap with you?"

He shrugged again. "Nothing, either you want to or you don't."

I shook my head "That's the worst sales pitch I ever heard. And that's bad because if you get out of here, you're going to need a job and sales is the only industry that's hiring. That and OnlyFans. Although you don't get hired on OnlyFans, it's just something that you do."

"What's OnlyFans?"

I snorted "Okay, so I'm supposed to think that you've been here for decades? This equipment does look old; that's nice window dressing. Is this like a pop-up escape room? Some kind of guerrilla theater? Is this an independent film about existential crap? I'll sign a waiver for five hundred dollars."

He straightened up again and stretched for a moment before going back to his counter-slouch "Look man, I have literally nothing to do so I'll talk to you for a long as you want, but I've had this conversation a million times and I don't want to go through all this again. I don't have any answers for you and I don't care about convincing you, I don't want to talk about the rules of the cursed room. If you want to swap, great. If not, let's talk about something else or please leave."

"A million people have come in here?"

He waved away my point "You know what I mean."

I half-pointed "That book is modern, Fifty Shades came out . . . sometime semi-recently. It's, uh, a modern thing. And it probably was out for a while before they translated it to Spanish so that adds a few years."

"Someone left it here. Hey, you know, if you don't want to swap with me what would be cool is if you could bring me some books or magazines. A VCR and a TV and some tapes. That would really be cool."

I laughed a real laugh, a small one, but a real small one "So the haunted cursed room of mystery has electricity?"

"Yeah" he said with a very slight nod.

"I don't get it. Is this good footage for whatever social media thing you're doing? A mildly confused man? Are you going to drop a bucket of cow manure on me or what's the punchline?"

He cocked his head slightly "You know, there is one thing I could say if I wanted to convince you. You're immortal while you're here."

"Don't age immortal or can't be killed immortal?"

"The first one for sure, I haven't tried out the second one."

"Really? You've been trapped here since before the internet and you've never tried to kill yourself?"

He made a face "No, of course not, why would I do that? What kind of thing is that to say to a person?"

"Just seems to me that eternal boredom might lead to a suicide attempt. So, if I went back up the street and bought a gun at the gun store and came back down here and blasted you in the chest, what do you think would happen?"

"No idea. Would you do that if I said I wanted to find out?"

"No."

"What if I paid you?" he asked semi-snarkily.

"Hey, man, you're the one with the help wanted sign, don't break bad with me because I'm asking about money."

He held up his hands slightly in half-surrender apology. "You're right, my bad."

"All right," I said after a moment.

He dipped his head in a barely perceptible nod that made me realize that he thought I was saying "All right, I accept your apology".

"I mean all right, I'll do it."

"Do what?" his eyes widened slightly "Oh, you mean you'll swap with me?"

"Sure," I shrugged.

He looked at me for a moment before speaking again. "Okay. Okay. Okay. I need you to understand that this is real, man. This is not a joke. I need you to really agree to this if you want to do it. This is real." He held his hand out palm up and gestured strangely, "This is serious. Like, I need you to understand. I don't want to screw you over because you think this is a joke."

"Sure, but let's say that I do think this is a joke and then it turns out to be real, if you feel bad about it then we can just swap again."

A look crept onto his face like the one you get before you start to feel like you're about to throw up. "I don't . . . I don't think I have the fucking fortitude for that man. Sorry to curse, but . . . like once I'm free I don't think . . . I can't promise you that I won't just run, man. I wish I was strong enough to promise that but I can't."

"You don't seem that desperate to get out of here, you seem pretty casual about it."

His eyes locked onto the door "I just . . . once I'm out there . . ." he wiped at a tear with his wrist, "if you swap and you want to swap back, I'll try but I might just bolt, dude. I've been in here a long time. And it's not so bad really while I'm here but once I'm out there . . . asking me to come back, that's like asking someone to go back into prison. I need you to agree for real."

"Okay, I believe you, I agree."

He stared at me for another few seconds "I don't believe you. You'll never see your friends or family again. Why would you agree to that?"

"Hey, a job's a job."

# Help Wanted
## by Victoria Nemethvargo

Nobody goes down here. Everyone knows their way around upstairs, the party central of the city. But the basement was a no-go for everyone. Elijah had bet Alica a whole ounce of *something* that she wouldn't go down here and bring back a souvenir. She snuck Jackson with her, and me? I was sent down 20 minutes later to see if they were being chased or just chasing a high. The latter seemed more probable but given the heavy metal chains that blocked off the basement door, I took the 50$ Elijah offered and headed down. He did seem pretty worried, but maybe that *something* was just starting to make him paranoid.

The smell of rusted metal is rather pungent when there's so much to go around. Each turn was stained with water damage, yellow smoke from the cigarettes being passed around upstairs. Old pipes lined the building, drawing intricate lines across the walls. The bass-boosted speakers from the party above echoed a dull thud through the underground section of the place. The vibrations made the peeling wallpaper swing as it hung from the ceiling.

"You both know I hate it here!" I called out into the hall. Jackson and Alicia really talked up this little event, begged me to come and promised a fun filled night. A great party, I'd been told, I couldn't miss it for the world! What they called fun filled, I found out to be getting high on nicotine and whatever else was in the electric pen Elijah brought. A great party had turned out to be old club songs from the 2000's drumming into your bones, college cheerleaders dancing on dirty tables, all surrounded by boys begging them to take their shirts off. As it turns out I could have missed this for almost anything and would have been better off.

A giggle echoed down the hallway to my left. I turned towards the sound and froze, waiting for another one. God, they really went deep into the maze of a basement now, didn't they? A second sound came, a sharp clang of something being dropped and hitting one of the rusted pipes.

"Gotcha, bitch" I muttered as I started towards the sound. Alicia was as clumsy as a baby giraffe, especially around Jackson. She probably dropped her phone or something, shaking hands fumbling for a light. I imagine it didn't take long to realize it was more fun to be with Jackson in the dark. I try not to let it bother me, pushing down memories of him being mine first, but all I manage to do is once again wonder:

Why am I even here?

I pulled out my phone to try to call them, wondering why I hadn't in the first place. Not surprisingly, I found no signal and let out a huff of indignation before shoving the thing back in the pocket of my jeans. I turned on my heel to go back the way I came. Maybe I could just sneak past Elijah, he would never know I didn't find them. Or maybe I could simply say they were just making out in the dark, like high school kids after prom. Tell him I didn't want to stay for the show. Just as I went round the left turn, I heard it again, a faint giggle from the dark door at the end of the hallway.

Peeking back around, I saw a light at the end of the hall that was once shrouded in darkness. My eyes narrowed a bit, wondering if they really were trying to scare me. If they were really on the other side of the door giggling away, turning the hall light on from the inside like porch lights on Halloween. It flickered a bit, though I suppose I should be grateful it worked at all. Unless, of course, I walk down this hallway only to have the light snuffed out again.

I run my hand absentmindedly down the brick walls as I walk, and the further I go, the colder they seem to feel. I scream as something scurries across my foot, seeing the rat after I jump back into my skin. My breath came out shaky as I tried to catch it, but it danced away from me to the beat of the music that was ever-fading. I turned my eyes back to the door and started to wonder if my curiosity was really worth this. Then the giggle came again, and the light flickered brighter, almost tauntingly.

"It's just a damn door," I muttered again, "and a big ass rat."

Standing right in front of the door, there was no sound, except a low whistle of wind I wasn't sure should be blowing down here. The handle was rusted over, but with a shine underneath as if it was once a palace gate. The paint was pristine and uncracked, just hidden in a layer of dust with cobwebs circling the corners. A single sign hung in the center of the door by rusted nails beat in at uneven angles.

"Help Wanted, Inquire Within"

The penmanship was the most beautiful I'd ever seen. The white paper was unwrinkled, unscorned apart from the nails that matched the rest of this place. But this paper did not match a single thing down here. The elegant scrawl was something of a fairytale, one my mother would have read to me before she left when I was 8. The golden letters seemed to glow, reflecting a sun that didn't exist.

A quick, thoughtless decision was made. I wasn't thinking about the consequences of opening the door, or what might be behind it. I wasn't thinking about the rats that stopped following me about 7 feet back. Maybe I was thinking about my mom leaving. Maybe I was thinking about Jackson's tongue down Alicia's throat. Maybe I wasn't really thinking at all, but at that moment, my hand met the cold metal of the doorknob.

I jerked away quickly as a rat squeaked from behind me before I could completely close my hand around the handle. I looked and tried to adjust my eyes to the black creature in the ever-dimming lights. It stood a good bit back, raised to its hind legs. And he stared at me, unmoving. For a moment, his eyes warned me, just before the giggle played out again from behind the door. With a final firm decision, I twisted the handle open.

Curiosity killed the cat, but the big ass rat seems to be doing just fine.

The knob turned with ease despite the rust that left maroon streaks down my palm. The door itself was, however, heavier than expected. I wondered if Alicia placed something in front of it to keep me out, like she expected me to come down and find them. I took a deep breath to shake the thought away, reminding myself I should feel worried, not envious. It doesn't work. With a furrowed brow, I try the door again.

Once again, it didn't budge.

I sucked in a quick breath as the door swung open from the other side.

"Well, are you coming in? The coffee is going to get cold, I've been keeping it on the heater for you."

The man eyed me with a small, playful smile, and I couldn't manage to make any words string together. My mind raced with a million questions that I couldn't get out. I could feel my jaw going slack in shock and heard my heartbeat in my ears.

"You are still interested in the position, correct?" His voice was hesitant, like he was worried I would say no. Position? What position?

I glanced back over to the sign nailed into the wood, the elegant scrawl suddenly clicking into place. What kind of job is even down here? The parties upstairs are all that has happened in the building for years now, and they are nothing if not unprofessional and unsupervised. The man before me wore solid black, with the top buttons of his dress shirt left undone. The thick golden watch stuck out brilliantly from the right hand he had leant on the doorframe above my head.

The parties. Alicia. Jackson. Are they in here? Maybe this is all a poorly written joke, maybe I'm just a punchline. If I let myself overthink it, it might just be the reason they even invited me here.

I nodded my head at the man without thinking about it; my mind was already running down the corridor with the rats. My legs just didn't follow suit. I raised my eyes to meet his fully for the first time. I barely bit back a reaction. His left eye was solid white, except for the red scar that bled a bit into the outer corner. His right was such a dark brown it looked black, and the contrast was jarring.

His smile was as bright as his left eye, teeth perfectly aligned like the cursive handwriting on the door. He stepped back and gestured for me to step inside, ducking his head a bit, but never losing the sideways grin. A strand of black hair fell heavy into his eyes, breaking from the mold a generous amount of gel had created. Without knowing why, I stepped into the doorway and entered.

The lights here didn't flicker. The smell of rust and wet pipes was gone and replaced by suffocatingly dry air. The only sound was a faint hum that I couldn't get a direction on. I heard the door click firmly behind me and spun to see the man directly behind me. I tried to move back a step but his hand caught my waist quickly. He had to bow his head to look at me and that smile returned. His eyes moved back to something behind me.

"She's just starting, let's not get ahead of ourselves. Introduce yourself properly, no need to frighten her." He spoke softly but firmly, in a tone that was undoubtedly in control of whomever or whatever he was speaking to.

He spun me around but kept me close, his chest pressing lightly into my back. It felt natural and familiar, like a path I had walked a million times even if I can't recall it. The heat radiating off of him did not ease the chill that went down my spine at the sight before me.

A young girl, no more than 6, stood swaying in a white sundress. Her blonde hair laid beautifully, her shoes shining brilliantly in the dim light, almost polished. She smiled crooked at me, tilting her head with a small giggle. I could feel my heartbeat in my throat. That was most definitely the giggle from the winding halls to get here.

"Oh, come on, it gets so lonely down here." She whined mockingly, "Is she here to play with us?"

The man stepped around me, and I felt the heat follow him, leaving me feeling cold from the inside out. His hand reached to ruffle her hair, but she quickly dodged him and took off down the hall to the right. He smiled after her before turning once more to me.

"Now that path will lead to the controls of, well, this side of the curtain. That is where you start. I'd love for you to excel and quickly move down the left path," he gestures, "and work more closely with me."

I took a deep breath and dug my voice out from its hiding place. "What exactly is this, this job for?" I ask as steadily as possible.

His reaction tells me my voice wasn't steady at all. The man chuckles a bit, a deep sound that feels like it echoes in the room. He looked down as he fiddled with his watch, seeming to adjust the time.

"I do apologize if Kylie startled you a bit, though it was her intention. I promise she is not always like this. Doing all the work alone has been difficult, so to speak. I don't have much time for her..." he trailed off a bit. I tried to focus on the words that were being spoken, but the hum was growing louder. My brain jogged to catch up, but kept getting winded. The pieces it put together didn't seem to answer my question at all. His eyes raised to mine as he walked over towards me. I felt like I should step back, but for some reason, I didn't.

"That is of course, where you come in my dear."

"What is she doing down here? Is she your daughter?"

"Don't worry about Kylie." His voice was strong, final. He gracefully laid an arm across my shoulders, gentle but unyielding as he guided me down the hall. I should feel uncomfortable,

I should find the door I came in and run back down to the party. I should have found-

I should have found Alicia and Jackson.

I stalled my footing and halted about midway down the path he was taking me, confused as I hadn't realized we had walked so far. I look behind me and the original door is further away than the room the little girl took off to. I shake the thought away and look at the man. When my eyes find him, he is already staring intently down at me.

"Something the matter darling? Your coffee is definitely cold by now, it's waiting for you on your desk." he spoke shortly, eyes unwavering. His breath fanned my face, sending an intoxicating waft mint gum through my senses. I pull my thoughts together to ask.

"I was looking for my friends, two of them. A boy and a girl, that's why I was down here. Did you see them, or hear them?"

He cocked his eyebrow down at me, a small quirk tugging on the corner of his lips.

"I've just been waiting for you, but I'm sure your friends are all right." He spoke softly, like he wanted to comfort me. But in the same notion, his tone was sharp like he wanted me to drop the subject.

I hadn't realized he had, started walking us again until I felt the floor drop a bit, throwing us onto a plush carpet. I felt myself sinking into the floor, and instinctively grabbed his arm; Afraid of sinking into the bottom of the ocean I felt like I was wading in. The sigh he let out bled a satisfactory tone, hitching my breath as I realized action. He chuckled softly again, and I tried to decide if I found it domineering or condescending.

"My dear, I assure you, nothing bad will happen to you here. I think you'll find staying with me to be most pleasing. Come now, sit down. I can show you what you're expected to do."

His hands guided me further into the small room, where a desk sat with a single cup of coffee on the corner. He walked me around to the far side and sat me before a line of watches. They were all different sizes, ticking at different speeds, or not ticking at all. I looked up to him, not feeling any less confused, but waiting for an explanation. He leaned down over my shoulder and ghosted his hands over a pink toned watch, with a white inlay and hands frozen at 7:33.

"This one suits you best, darling. Here, let's see it on you."

The chair was quickly spun and I let out a small yelp. His eyes narrowed, not angry, almost amused. Something in the back of my mind told me to move away, but my body wasn't listening. He took my wrist gently into his hands, radiating a heat that should have burned or at least been uncomfortable. Somehow it wasn't, and a thought that wasn't mine to lean into the heat unnerved me. The watch was quickly clasped around my wrist, almost too tight but feeling like something I've always had there.

Something like a memory flashes just out of sight, and somewhere in the missing pieces, the watch is mine.

"Beautiful." he whispered, cocking his head up to face my eyes. "I told you this one suits you." He continued before standing up and stepping back abruptly. His eyes danced behind me. When I turned to see why, the little girl was back. I hadn't heard her come in.

"What color is her watch? Did she pick one yet? How much time has she got?" The girl asked the man questions in a rapid-fire style, seeming to forget to breathe in between the inquiries. He sighed at her lightly, and she giggled at the irritation she caused. The lights in the room brightened as she laughed but soon returned to their normal dimmed appearance.

"Kylie, don't ask so many questions before she is ready. Go play, she will be ready soon enough." The man scolded her in a way that reminded me of a brother. The older ones who think they control the world. I suppose here, in this basement of watches, he does.

The little girl scurried off without another word, and her footsteps ran out silently into the hall. I feel his hand brush the side of my hair gently back to rest behind my shoulder and I lean slightly into it before realizing the move I made. My mouth dries up, like I stuffed it full of cotton candy at a fair. I risk a look up at him and meet his eyes already staring down at me. He smiles wider than he should, unblinking as he praises me for it.

"You're going to be great here, darling. Don't worry about a thing down here. Just select some watches—not for you but rather, whichever ones speak to you." My eyes flickered between the watches in front of me and the man.

"Select them for what, exactly? What am I looking for?"

"Don't overthink this, darling. I can see it in you, you will do great work with us. The right watches will show themselves, if you simply allow them to."

Without another word, he floats down the hall, seemingly unbothered about how little I understand or how many of my questions he didn't answer.

Unsure of what else to do, I looked to the watches in front of me. Some silver plated, some gold. A few of them were rusted over and hadn't been cared for in what looked like decades. Others were children's watches, digital faces with bright colors or cartoon characters decorating the bands.

With a furrowed brow, I gently took one into my right hand. Maybe inspecting them will help? The moment it rested flat on my palm, a scream echoed from a direction I couldn't decipher.

*How many times have I told you to close the damn gate!*

I dropped the watch with a yelp, quickly moving to survey my surroundings. Nobody was here or in the hall. There were no windows or other doorways. There were no more screams. My eyes fell back onto the rows of watches, lined up and ticking away. To disprove the incredulous thought, I gently picked up a second watch- A golden pocket watch with a military insignia engraved on the cover.

With a deep breath, I laid it flat onto my palm.

This one was quieter. A faint rumble of a tank driving overhead. An echo of a bomb and screams from fellow soldiers. A man praying to see his wife again. The echoes were faint, but they were there. I set the watch down and looked at the rest of the table. My eyes drifted and lingered on the 4th from the left, in the 3rd row.

I know this one.

The heavier black metal, the golden inlay with the roman numerals instead of typical numbers. The hands were thin and fine, giving the watch an overall strong but gentle look. I remembered seeing it at the mall with Alicia 2 years ago, and I remembered buying it for Jackson's birthday the year we graduated. I remembered throwing this watch at the wall, and the cracks it left down the face, repairable but never done. I suppose because Jackson never cared much for it, or me for that matter. The bastard still wore it, but that's neither here nor there.

Except it is here, with the same cracks in the face I made 2 years ago. I picked the watch up, expecting my hands to shake but finding them completely steady. I ran my finger over the same imperfections, the glass lightly tugging at the skin of my fingertips like a threat. I flipped the watch around, looking for the engraving I'd paid for.  And there it was.

Jackson Price

Like the others, I rested the watch lightly on the center of my palm. The echo was more than a voice, it was a feeling. I heard myself screaming Jackson's name, I felt my anger, his regret. I fought back the bubble that was expanding in my chest, weighing down my lungs.

I stood up quickly, my lungs filling with air at a speed I didn't know they could reach. The lightheaded, airy feel to this place was gone. It felt like I was breathing in smoke from a house fire. And all the alarms were sounding, just in my own head instead of from a ceiling monitor with decade old batteries. My eyes scanned the room wildly, suddenly realizing there was nothing else here. This desk, these watches, and the hall in front of me. The coffee remained untouched yet steaming on the corner. The walls seemed closer to me than they were before.

In a quick decision, I move to make my way to the door. Kylie greets me there.

"It's pink! No fair, I got a purple one with Paul Frank monkeys on it! He knows I don't like purple. I think he likes you more," the girl pouts, firing questions a mile a minute like she had to the man before.

I try to chase my focus and pin it down to her words, but half of me is still frozen in the chair holding Jackson's watch.

"I like yours, Kylie. Mine is pink, but it is very simple. And rather noisy." I try to jest with the girl and in that moment, I want to take her with me. I wonder if anyone is looking for her. Her eyes are a strong green when she looks up at me, almost brighter than grass on a summer solstice.

"Mine doesn't even tick anymore. See? A pink one would work." She speaks with annoyance as she thrusts her wrist out, the small watch frozen at 5:28. Without thinking, I reach my hand out and brush over the face. And for a moment, I can hear it, the sharp crack of a toy shattering on a wall. An angry mother shouting Kylie's name. My heart aches for the girl in front of me. I look back down at my own watch, and see that 7:33 has only moved to 7:38, but I am sure it's been longer, and I know I've heard more ticks than that.

"Kylie, why are you here? Do you work for him?" I ask lightly, keeping to mind that I am talking to a child, although part of me feels like I'm not.

She giggles again, and 3 watches from the table start buzzing, different timers going off at different frequencies. I look towards them reflexively, but when I return to the hall, Kylie is gone. I look at Jackson's watch, and even through the broken glass see the hands still ticking, though quieter than mine. I step into the hallway, leaving the watch room behind, and imagine myself pushing forward. Pushing through the rest of this hall, making it to the door, and following the rats' warnings. Alicia and Jackson can't possibly be in here, there was only coffee for me.

Each step down the hall is like dragging my feet through quicksand. My head starts pounding, a bruising headache forming to the beat of the ticking echoing off of my wrist. The walkway feels narrow and cold. No matter how far I walk, the end looks further away than the desk with the watches. My breath runs faster than I can, and I feel my chest getting heavier, pulling me to the floor. I feel my legs give out, my blood not carrying the oxygen they need to them because, well, I'm not taking in any oxygen.

Instead of the floor, I feel his arms around me.

"Now, darling, you could have waited for me, but I love to see the eagerness on you."

Hearing his voice again after him being gone feels intoxicating, but not euphoric in nature. It's more like taking a drink from a cup you left unattended and immediately knowing something is wrong. But then the euphoria kicks in, laced somewhere in the mint on his breath. He pulls me upright, leaving a firm hand on my waist as he tsks lightly at me.

"If you're sure you're ready to see the next part of the job, by all means, come with me. I do hope you enjoyed the coffee then, darling."

He speaks evenly, never wavering in tone, as he pulls me along with him down the hallway. With him here, the walls step back and the doorway rests and allows us to catch up. His hand stays locked on my waist, pressing me into his side and enveloping me in a warmth that seems to only come from him down here.

"What is this for? Why am I here?" It's the most words I've managed to get out all evening, and I can barely get them out. His presence is overwhelming, to say the least.

He stops us in the first room, and I see the door to the halls that lead to the parties. My gaze locks onto it, but he moves in front of me and captures my focus again, clearing his throat.

"Now, darling, I thought this was gone over in the application process, but if it's escaped you, we can recap. You are mainly responsible for the selection process, the discovery of the watches that need my attention. The people out there," he points to the door, "are blind to us. They think they have all the options, but we guide the final life they lead." His words are sharp and direct, with a strong air of ego lacing them.

"Where are my friends? You've had to have seen them, if you're always here, if you control them." My words are meant to have power behind them but standing here I feel small. I barely whisper the questions, my mind screaming at me to be quiet. He sighs again, not overly irritated, but rather tired. Like it's an effort to remind himself to lessen the bite in his words, to remind himself to coat them in sugary additives.

"Darling, what friends were they, exactly? You shouldn't trouble your thoughts with the likes of them. Come now, I assure you my company will be much more pleasurable, if you stop with all these questions."

He held his hand out for me to take, seeming to give me a choice. A scratching sounds from the door behind him, and I catch the tilted head of a rat, staring at me. Warning me. I felt my hand raise to meet the man's without my brain telling it to. The watch on my wrist ticked wildly as my hand connected to his, a satisfied huff leaving his lips as it did. The rodent at the door slumps on all fours, almost defeated. I move to pull my hand away, but the grip only tightens. Not enough to hurt, but enough to know it could. My eyes meet his, and he grins wide, holding my gaze for a moment before tugging me off down his hallway. I glance back just enough to see the thin tip of a tail slip underneath the door.

"Now, you seem to be picking up the run around here awfully quick, I am rather impressed. I think it's about time to show you the real gears that grind this place. You won't make many decisions, but you can certainly aid me in mine." His speech falls back into its business casual demeanor with ease. Each move he makes is as if he is unaffected by anything that can go wrong, any concerns I have. I am here to follow him, and he is fully content in that.

"What do you do here?" I ask lightly. This hall feels shorter than the other, and right as I get the question out, we arrive at a door. It's almost identical to the one I came into, but the paint is clean and there is no rust. There is no dust or debris. The door is impeccable.

"Go find out for yourself, darling." He gestures to the door. I hesitate, turning to look behind me, and seeing only a dark hall with no visible end. I see no other way out, and for a beat I wonder how I got so deep into this, without fully knowing what this is. I reach for the doorknob and twist it, feeling it fall open with ease in comparison to the last one.

The air felt purified, like I was breathing with new lungs. Everything looked ethereal, like even the air would shatter if I waved through it with rough hands. The room was much larger than mine, golden frames lining the walls, holding oil paintings that didn't look quite right. All of them shifted slightly as I walked by, never a clear image. I stopped at the 5th on the left wall, trying to focus on the scene before me. It only seemed to give me a headache, the man in the painting refusing to come into focus. He stood on the roadway of a busy city street, arm raised to the traffic. The white paint glowed and shimmered as if the cars in the painting were moving like real rush hour. Just to the right of the painting, a plaque rested with a name, age, and timestamp.

Ashton Willow, Aged 27, 8:52

My hands ghosted over the plaque, raised like a letter holder. Inside rested a single watch, ticking slowly like Jackson's had. I took it gently, seeing the time match the one on the wall. As I turned it over in my hand, I could faintly hear a call from a woman- calling Ashton's name from afar. He called back to her- *Bridget*. I could hear the smile in his voice. I felt uneasy without being able to place a cause, and a moment later felt the man's heat at my back. It shouldn't have calmed me.

It did.

He reached around my body and twisted the timer on the watch, speeding it up to 9:13. My eyes shifted to the plaque, where the timestamp had also changed. Hands found my arms, seeming to know the nausea was coming towards me. The painting began to move, brushstrokes rearranging as if it was a natural occurrence, gliding themselves over the canvas. The man was now home, hands resting on a bottle, seeming to contemplate the whiskey glass in front of him.

"What did you do?" I asked weakly, and in my mind I turned to face the man, demanding answers that weren't laced with honey and falsities. In reality, I felt myself lay gently into the warmth he provided, finding a sick comfort in the hands on my arms, in the understanding that he controlled everything here. In his promises that I wouldn't be hurt here.

"I took away a choice. He didn't get into the cab and meet the girl, he walked home to meet the bottle." the man spoke lightly, "now the bottle, that was his decision. But the girl, he wasn't allowed the option."

I turned out of his arms, the fact that he let me weighing heavy on my mind. Taking in the room, I realized there were easily hundreds of paintings here, some scattered up high to the ceiling, and ranging of many different sizes. Each had a plaque, presumably each holding a watch that barely ticked. I wondered how he kept an eye on all of them.

"You've selected one, haven't you? One that spoke to you?" he asked, business casual coming naturally in place to him. Confusion clouded my mind briefly before a realization dawned sharply.

Jackson's watch.

My breath hitched as the man pulled it from his pocket, narrowing his eyes at it in inspection. He spun lightly on his heel and headed to the opposite corner of the room, and I quickly followed pursuit. He stopped as I caught up enough to hear the light mutterings he let out to himself, kneeling down to a square painting close to the floor.

"Well, what do we have here? Darling, tell me, do we let him stay down here looking for you? If you would rather, I can send him on his way with that tramp he brought down here, it would buy him a few more revisions. Not many, but he will see his mother again before it happens."

His words hung heavy in an otherwise weightless room, holding my feet down a few paces back from where I'd almost met him at the wall.

Jackson is looking for me.

"Before… before what happens?" I ask, though in the pit of my stomach, I know. I know what happens to the man with the bottle, and I know what will happen to every watch in here that keeps slowing down.

The man raises to his feet, meeting me at my frozen place in two small strides. My jaw locks up when my eyes find the painting his body previously shielded. Jackson stood, in the maze of dirty halls, a glow of white paint depicting his flashlight, as water dripped from a rusted pipe. Rats tug at his shoelaces.

Warm fingers gently raise my head to look into the unmatched eyes of the man. His gaze is deep, drowning, hypnotic. The way he holds my stare feels as if he wants me to be lost in his presence. His voice echoes through me.

"He won't find you. Not in time. I can give him more time, darling, if you'd like. Say the word."

I felt my jaw slack, my breath escaping shakily like a panic attack waiting to happen. My eyes wildly searched his but only found a rock to pull myself deeper into the dark ocean he created. I felt his thumb brush just below my cheek, an exhalation of mint cooling the heat rising to my face as he shushed me gently, the way one would console a child.

My words came out choked, hyperventilation lining them.

"Please, please give him more time."

The man smirked crookedly down at me. "Good girl. Not too difficult, is it?" he stepped back and turned the dial on Jackson's watch, and my eyes stung as I watched the paint on his image dance away from the hallways, and back upstairs to the party I'd left.   The watch was placed in the slot behind the plaque, and I scanned the age and timestamp listed there.

Jackson Price, Aged 21, 11:11

"Now, darling, I believe you've got quite the grasp on everything here. Do you have any questions? To reiterate, you will mainly be functioning in your own office, selecting the watches that speak, and delivering them to me here. Typically, the decisions on this end are mine, but I do appreciate the company. Especially if that company brings coffee." His tone slipped back into its usual, unbothered, business casual. It was as if nothing had just conspired between us, as if we hadn't just discussed the lifeline of two people. The whiplash was jarring, and I found myself unable to speak. Questions- I had a million of those.
        "You are very promising, I can tell you that. I'd loathe to burn you out, why don't we rest for a bit?" he reached his hand towards me, eyeing me expectantly.

I felt lightheaded. A million questions raced inside my mind. I manage to ask one of them.

"I'm never getting out of here, am I?"

The man smiled crooked again, closing the space between us. His hand took mine from my side as I moved my head to watch the motion. Holding it in between us at chest level, he used his other hand to fiddle with the dial on my watch, before bending down to place a kiss on the tips of my knuckle.

"Darling, you're in a bit too deep to be worried about the surface."

# Echoes of the Forgotten

by Ashleigh Norris

The corridor was a study in contrasts. To the right, rough brick whispered tales of the building's age, each groove a tiny shadow. To the left, peeling plaster hinted at forgotten attempts to modernize, to smooth over the past. At the end, bathed in a sickly green glow, was the door. Above it, a faded sign, its original message lost to time, loomed like a forgotten memory. Below, stark and freshly painted, the words blazed: "HELP WANTED - INQUIRE WITHIN."

Eliza hesitated. The air hung thick with the scent of dust and something else, something metallic and faintly unsettling. She'd stumbled upon this place by accident, a wrong turn in a city she barely knew. The promise of a job was a beacon, but the setting... it felt like a dare. Desperate, she reached out, her fingers brushing the cool, slick paint of the sign. A tremor ran through her.

Taking a breath, Eliza pushed the door open. A bell, long disused, gave a rusty jingle. The green light intensified, revealing a small, cluttered office. Behind a mountain of papers sat a woman with eyes as sharp as shards of glass. "Took you long enough," the woman said, her voice a low rasp. "We've been waiting." Eliza stepped inside, the door creaking shut behind her, sealing her fate in the heart of the unknown.

The woman gestured to a chair buried under a pile of ledgers. "Sit. We need to know what you're good at." Eliza cleared the chair, the dust motes dancing in the green light. "I... I'm a fast learner," she stammered, "and I'm good with people."

The woman raised a skeptical eyebrow. "People are overrated. Can you keep secrets? Can you follow instructions, no matter how strange?"

Eliza swallowed, the metallic scent growing stronger. "Yes," she said, though a knot of unease tightened in her stomach. "I can."

"Good." The woman leaned forward, her gaze intense. "Our organization... we deal with things others can't. Lost things. Forgotten things. Things that shouldn't be." She paused, letting the words sink in. "Your first task: there's a package in the back. Bring it to me. Don't open it. Don't ask questions."

Eliza hesitated, but the desperation in her own life outweighed her fear. She nodded and turned toward a dark doorway at the back of the office. As she stepped into the shadows, she couldn't shake the feeling that she was walking into something far more dangerous than she could ever imagine.

The back room was colder, the air heavy with the scent of decay. Moonlight filtered through a grimy window, illuminating shelves crammed with oddities: dusty books bound in strange leather, glass jars filled with murky liquids, and antique tools with unknown purposes. In the center of the room, on a rickety table, sat a small, wooden box bound with iron. It hummed faintly, a vibration that tickled Eliza's fingertips as she picked it up.

As instructed, she didn't open it, but the box felt strangely warm, almost alive. Back in the office, the woman watched her approach, her eyes gleaming in the green light. "Put it on the desk," she commanded. Eliza obeyed, placing the box carefully on the cluttered surface. The humming intensified, and the room seemed to vibrate in response.

The woman reached out, her fingers tracing the iron bands. "Excellent," she murmured. "You've passed the first test." She looked up at Eliza, a strange smile playing on her lips. "Now, for the second..." She pulled a small, silver key from her pocket and held it out. "Open it."

Eliza hesitated, remembering the woman's warning: "Don't ask questions." But curiosity gnawed at her. "What's inside?" she blurted out before she could stop herself. The woman's smile widened, but it didn't reach her eyes. "That's not for you to know," she said, her voice hardening. "Your job is to follow instructions. Open the box."

Swallowing her apprehension, Eliza took the key. It was cold and heavy in her hand. She inserted it into the tiny lock on the box, her fingers trembling slightly. With a click, the lock sprung open. Eliza lifted the lid, peering inside. The box was lined with faded velvet and nestled within was a single object: a tarnished silver locket.

As Eliza reached for it, the woman grabbed her wrist. "Careful," she warned. "That locket... it holds memories. Powerful ones. Don't touch it unless I tell you to." Eliza stared at the locket, a strange pull emanating from it. It felt familiar, like a forgotten dream. "Whose memories?" she asked, her voice barely a whisper.

The woman's grip tightened. "That," she said, "is what we're going to find out."

The woman released Eliza's wrist and picked up the locket, holding it up to the green light. "This locket belonged to someone very special," she said, her voice softening. "Someone who lost their way." She opened the locket, revealing two tiny portraits: a young woman with fiery red hair and a man with kind eyes. "They were deeply in love," the woman continued, "but their love was forbidden."

As she spoke, the room began to shimmer, the air growing thick with energy. Eliza felt a strange pull, a sense of being drawn into the locket itself. The woman turned to her, her eyes glowing with an otherworldly light. "You see, Eliza," she said, "this locket is a gateway. A gateway to the past. And you... you are the key."

With a final, cryptic smile, the woman placed the locket in Eliza's hand. As their fingers touched, a surge of energy coursed through Eliza's body. The room dissolved around her, and she found herself standing in a sun-drenched meadow, the scent of wildflowers filling the air. In the distance, she saw two figures approaching, hand in hand. The woman with fiery red hair and the man with kind eyes. Their story, it seemed, was just beginning. And Eliza was now a part of it.

# Operator 917
by Samantha Oliver

They didn't ask for a résumé. Just a voice sample.

That should've been the first warning. But warnings don't pay rent. They don't keep the heat running or the fridge stocked. And they sure as hell don't help when your son's growing out of his shoes every other month.

So, when the job ad slid into view— plain text, no logo, just: ***NOW HIRING: NIGHT OPERATORS, NO EXPERIENCE NEEDED***— Carla clicked apply.

The office was squeezed between a pawn shop and a shuttered buffet. The door bore a single number: 917. Inside, it smelled faintly of bleach and something older. Sweet. Like rotting fruit beneath soap.
A woman behind the desk looked up and smiled— bright, unnatural teeth.
"You'll be taking calls," she said. "They come in. You answer. You log them. No names. No questions. And no matter what— don't touch Line 917."
Carla's eyes landed on the far corner of the call board. A red bulb. Unlit. The numbers beside it looked warped, like the plastic had softened under heat.
The woman didn't blink. "Understand?"
Carla nodded. "Yes."

The first week passed in a haze.
She read from the script. Logged each call. Most of the questions made no sense— "Yes, veil confirmations are still valid." The words meant nothing, but her mouth remembered them anyway.
Sometimes voices dropped mid-sentence, then resumed colder. Different.
She didn't ask. She needed the check.
At 9:17 each night, the red light blinked once.
And went dark.
She never touched it.

Her son got sick the second week.
The fever came fast— glass skin, burning eyes. The clinic handed her expired antibiotics in a plastic bag. No insurance. No help.
That night, Line 917 pulsed twice. Slow. Measured. Waiting.
Her hand hovered over the button.
Then it went dark.

By week three, she noticed the silence.
At first, she thought the others were on break. Then a day passed. Then two. Their chairs stayed pushed back, headsets limp on their hooks like forgotten tools. The woman at the desk was gone. A man now stood in her place— charcoal suit, clipboard in hand. He didn't look up. Didn't speak.
Carla took her seat.
That night, Line 917 didn't blink.
It held.
One second. Two. Five.
She stared. Then pressed it.
"Operator," she said.
A breath answered. Damp, slow. Like someone exhaling through frostbitten lips.
"Thank you," the voice said.

It was her own.
But not quite. Slowed. Echoed. Pulled from somewhere deep.
"Thank you for letting me in."
The line cut.

The next morning, her son was fine.
He sat cross-legged in front of the TV, eating eggs and laughing. His cheeks were warm. Eyes clear. The pills sat unopened on the counter.
"I heard you talking last night," he said.
Carla froze. "What?"
He kept eating. "But you weren't home."

The board was empty when she returned.
Except for Line 917.
It blinked. Once. Then again.
At 9:17, a rotary phone rang on her desk. She didn't remember it being there when she sat down.
It wasn't plugged in.
It rang anyway.
The man in the suit walked in. Nodded.
She picked it up.
"Hello?"
A pause. Then:
"You weren't supposed to leave."
It was her voice again. But hollow. Thinned out like a copy of a copy.
Her reflection in the dark monitor behind the board lagged half a second behind.
She hung up.
The phone rang again.
She pulled the cord from the wall.
It kept ringing.

She didn't return the next night.
But the door at 917 opened for someone else.
A young woman stepped in. Early twenties. Eyes dull with fatigue.
Behind the desk sat Carla.
Hair pulled back. Blouse pressed. A silver pin on her collar.
She smiled— wide, too white.
"You'll be taking calls," she said. "They come in. You answer. You log them. No names. No questions. And no matter what—"
She gestured toward the board.
Line 917 blinked once.

**"Don't touch that one."**

# Behind the Counter
## by Lynda Vann

I have two things on my mind: going home tonight and finding someone that wants to apply for a job at Film Galore. The manager, Jerry McDonald, has been on my case for weeks hoping to find a new co-worker for me to "be friends" with.

Jerry means well, I know he does.

He just doesn't want me to work the cash register alone, especially at night.

I always end up working a little after my shift ends since I'm the only one usually willing to stick around and he always says "walking home alone" is dangerous as if I'm going to be kidnapped tomorrow. He figured having a "buddy" joining me on the night shift would make things easier for me and give me someone to talk to. But that's why he's the boss, right? Gotta do what he says.

Anyway, I always carry pepper spray.

I enjoy working at Film Galore. I've been here for a year and it's definitely the right fit for me as a film and video game enthusiast. My favorite films are usually about cryptids, thrillers, and romance. Learning about mythical creatures like Yeti, Bigfoot, the Skunk Ape, and the stories behind these different creatures is what made me want a job in a movie store to begin with.

Growing up in Florida, my mom always read stories to me when I was little, typical children's stories like "Are You My Mother?" by P. D. Eastman but also the book that started my love of cryptids: "Nessie, Baby" by Elias Barks and Zoe Persico.

After reading that, I wanted to know all about the Loch Ness monster, where it originated from, what it looks like, any sightings, and I felt more enthralled seeing cryptids like that in public than an alligator (you get used to it after a while).

Venturing into the paranormal was not scary for little gap-toothed 8 year old Penelope Garcia. In a way I felt seen by those creatures, rare, yet deeply misunderstood by everyone. Those monsters were my friends on paper. Being bullied in elementary school definitely made me feel that way but grow through what you go through, right?

People would laugh and say I was such a "nerd" for being too enthusiastic about the paranormal and cryptids. Reading about them soothed me and blocked out the noise of the bullies. Watching movies about them intensified my fan obsession! Seeing how different film directors imagined the Yeti, Loch Ness monster, Bigfoot, and Wendigos only provided comfort in times of distress. Finally, other people saw my vision and were interested. As long as I had my movies and books, I was happy.

Which landed me my job at Film Galore 10 years later. It is my first job out of high school. I needed this job as my family had been struggling to pay the bills and I needed something productive to do instead of being home all summer long. I applied to multiple jobs, got rejected by most of them, except for Film Galore. Jerry saw something in me since the first day. Although, now he playfully shoos me away when I get carried away talking about the new movies we can add to inventory.

"Penny-pie, I know how much you love all that mythical stuff and movies but I need someone up front to keep this store running!" Jerry says playfully, heading back to his office holding files and paperwork.

"Penny-pie," I smile softly. His little nickname for me, he always says he sees me as a second daughter. His *real* daughter, Shelby, was busy living with her mother for the summer in Oregon and I know he misses her. He always talks about me meeting her one day; she is also a movie fanatic according to him. He says he'd help arrange a movie hangout once she comes back to Florida in the fall.

I appreciated his kindness and his companionship.  He knew my life has not been easy and helping him recruit potential workers is the least I can do for him.

"Any luck finding anyone interested in working here?" He walks into his office and sits down in his big black rolling chair, tapping his fingers pensively.

His office was very simplistic in that all four walls were white, a framed movie poster of Jaws on the left hand side across from this was his desk, a wooden dark maroon colored desk with four drawers and a polished surface. On his desk was a slightly old dusty working computer.

"Nope! I tried asking Aimee but she's set on working as a camp counselor for kids with disabilities."

Aimee was my best friend, my only friend, that I met freshman year of high school. She accepted my love for cryptids as I accepted her love for Beanie Babies. Our friendship was simple: I scratch her back and she scratches mine.

Okay, maybe she scratches mine a lot more because she would quickly defend me if anyone tried to mess with me. She was short but mighty. She wants to become an occupational therapist after graduation and I can't stop her from doing what's best for her, even though eating popcorn and having conversations about video games and anime is considered best in my book.

Jerry sneers then laughs. "You know she's a go-getter!"

"I know, I know. Besides, I'll be fine. I know how to work the cash register, even with my eyes closed." I joked.

"I trust ya', kid." Jerry says. "Now, go—people will be coming in any minute.  You don't want to be here all night, do you?"

"Don't have to tell me twice!" As much as I loved working here, I did want to go home for two simple reasons: to rot in bed under the covers to watch conspiracy videos and sleep.

I was starting to get caught up on conspiracy theories with this YouTube channel called "The Crypto Coons" featuring Brad Stacey and Laci Surman. They have a new series on cryptozoological creatures.  Last week they covered the Beast of Bladenboro, an angry cat-like creature found in North Carolina with a deafening screech allegedly attacking dogs and wildlife and supposedly draining the blood of horses as its main course. Now it's Florida's turn. I wanted to see what they were going to cover next; my guess was the Skunk Ape or Old Hitler.

I hurriedly run over to the cash register and greet the guests as they enter, letting the time pass as it did. Closing time rolls around and I'm surely beat. I clock out and wish Jerry goodbye as I head out and on my way home.

I walk home carrying my key in between my fingers and my alarm on standby. Can't be too easygoing. I live around ten blocks away from my job and I can't be bothered to constantly ask my mom for a ride as that usually comes at the price of listening to her turn my jokes into life lessons. Walking is exercise, so it's got to be good for me, right?

I'm reflecting on my day — okay, I know what you're thinking back on. It's the Old Hitler thing, isn't it? It's just some old tale from when my mom lived in Tampa during her teen years. She says Old Hitler was a giant seventeen foot long hammerhead shark that would show up during the summer to eat other sharks and tarpon. Of course, Mom never actually saw him and according to her, he's just "too strong and can't be messed with." I don't know about that, Mom. People mess with alligators all the time here, would it really be any different? Who knows?

I like the comfort of my job and I feel like having a co-worker might stress me out since I'm used to Jerry always relying on me, but I guess it would be nice to have a pupil to teach. A master and apprentice duo, if you will. Someone to talk to.

Today, people aren't interested in talking more than the normal pleasantries of "How are you?" or "Fine weather we're having," although this one old lady did give me advice on how to not burn the popcorn as she was deciding on what movie to get her grandson.

I sighed, dropping my shoulders to release the tension. Another day, another dollar.

I reach the front of my apartment and quickly head into the elevator, glancing over my shoulder to make sure nobody is following. I opened the door to my apartment, closed the door, kicked off my shoes and fell into my bed. I'm exhausted. I scroll through my phone and change into my pajamas ready to tune into the Crypto Coons. Mom, who is an ER nurse, is out working a late night shift in the hospital so it'll just have to be me and my bed. Home alone. One of the many small things to live for in life.

No matter what time I drift off to sleep, I always wake up in the middle of the night. My body clings to the last bit of my dreams before I wake and realize I'm not lucid dreaming. My vision is blurry and my brain is still half asleep.

Work, work, work. Out of all the random things I could think about, it just so happens to be that. Normally, that line of thinking would add to my anxiety and stress, but I believe I've solved our conundrum of having people not apply for a job at Film Galore. See, people need to feel inspired to do something. Everyone is motivated by something: money, prestige, success, failure, etc. We need to make our "Looking for employment? Sign up Here!" poster more appealing. "Help Wanted, Inquire Within!" sounds more mysterious. I grab an empty poster and write out "Help Wanted! Inquire Within!" with a few aesthetic designs, just to really set the mood. Nothing signifies a video store more than a camera, popcorn, and movie. I stare at my glorious masterpiece and sit on my bed quietly, looking around at my room.

I feel like ever since high school ended, I have too much time on my hands that I don't know what to do with all of it. It's starting to make me question the concept of time. Is it even real? Is it relevant? Is it on my side? Eh, I don't know.

I look at my pastel pink walls decorated with lilac flowers and sunflower LED lights hanging around the corners of my walls. The other side of my room has all my movie posters and drawings of different mythical creatures, one of them being a drawing of the Skunk Ape that I received as a birthday gift from Aimee. My tv on my antique white dresser, pitch black. My feet planted on the white fluffy rug feeling cozy. This is me in my space. In all of its glory.

I lay back down snuggling into my blanket and drift off to sleep before my alarm rings.

I get ready for work and pick up my poster. Mom is in the kitchen with a cup of coffee in her hands.

"I'm sorry I missed you last night, work was hectic" she says as I walk over to her.

"Mom, it's okay! You know me," I chuckle. "I just go to my room to do my thing and make dinner when I need to," I smile.

I wanted her to know that I was growing into my independence and that she didn't need to hover over me constantly anymore.

"Oh, I know. You're my grown little woman. You know moms just worry. You never know what's out there." She voiced worriedly, her brows furrow.

"You know I've never been afraid of what's out there, I could find a Yeti wanting to be my friend!" I joke, bracing for a lecture.

Instead, she just laughs, "Or make friends with Old Hitler passing by the lake." She gave me a wide grin.

Some days that was just our dynamic, my jokes were either going to be jokes or a lecture.

I turn the knob and head out to work when she interrupts "Nice poster, love. You've always been the creative one! Now, be safe."

"But how did you — ?"

"I noticed it when I came home, I came into your room to check up on you and you were sleeping."

"Thank you, Mama! Didn't realize Edward Cullen was in the house."

Moms really do notice everything.

While at work, I showed Jerry the post to see if he'd give me permission to put it up next to the official posters of the place outside.

He looks at me with a "if you think this will work, go for it" look. "Sure, why the hell not?"

"Seriously? I thought you'd consider it childish or stupid or —"

"Penny-pie." he interrupts, placing a delicate hand on my left shoulder, "I believe in you, best believe I mean that. Plus, you're young and hip! If you know what will attract more applicants, by all means…do it."

My smile stretched wide, a constellation of joy in my eyes. "Thanks, Jerry! I won't let you down," the words bubbling out, infused with hopeful promise. I hurriedly walk outside to put up the poster with an excited feeling in my stomach and grin widely.

Yes, yes, yes! We'll finally put this baby in action. Now we wait. I walk back inside the store and almost spring behind the counter to set up the cash register for the day. I'm ignoring the fact that he said "young and hip," by the way, just because I'm so excited!

*One week passes.*

Some people expressed interest in the poster and application, applauding me for my creativity. We even had one person apply, they had their interview, but Jerry had a bad feeling and that he can sense someone's work ethic based on how they're dressed.

"You gotta dress for success, y'know, Penny-pie?" I recall him saying with his usual laid-back accent.

"I guess so, Jerry"

"This may be retail, but retail is the start of forever! It's a job that sticks with you even when you retire, ya' don't forget how it made you feel."

"I hear you. Don't worry, we'll get more people to apply soon. It's all just a part of the process. I mean, you did get on my case for weeks about this, so beggars can't be choosers!" I playfully nudged him on the arm.

"Yeah, yeah, yeah. You know what I mean." He goes back into his office to do more paperwork and I go return stock the snack aisle while keeping an eye on the register.

I stand in front of the snacks aisle, adding more snacks and candies that we received from inventory. I reach for the bag of Doritos and place it on the top shelf, slightly getting on my tippy toes. I'm loading up the Crunch bars when I hear a sound behind me.

"Hello, do you work here?"

I slowly turn around and my world narrowed to the man standing before me, every detail of him demanding my full attention.

This guy is absolutely handsome. He's around nineteen, a couple of inches taller than me, with light brown hair swept down slightly over his face and honey-brown eyes. He looks like a young James Marsden or a brown-eyed Jeremy Sumpter.

I blink a few too many times and try to regain my composure, "Oh, hi! How can I help you?" I grin sheepishly.

He motions over to the "Help Wanted! Inquire Within!" poster with his finger and side eyes me. "I saw your sign."

"Ha,ha, right, right." I feel myself getting nervous, my palms sweating. I laugh nervously and avert my eyes slightly.

Moments of silence between us.

"So," he begins. "How do I apply?"

My lips curved. "Welllll," I drew out the word, a playful lilt in my voice. "You apply online at the Film Galore website and my boss, Jerry, will look at your application, then—hopefully—you'll hear from him soon."

"Cool, cool! Guess I'll go about doing that then."

"Cool. It'd be fun to work together…in a store like this, ha-ha." I'm digging a hole in my grave. Bury me in the coffin of embarrassment!

"It would be. I love movies." He smiles, his captivating gaze holding mine. Goodness, even his smile is attractive.

"Same! I mean why else would I be here?" I stutter over my words.

"For the snacks, probably," he jokes.

I look down and notice the Crunch bar still in my hand. "Ha, ha, ha, you got me there…?" I say, motioning to question what his name is.

"Alexander," he smiles, "Alexander Kirby."

"Penelope. Penelope Garcia." I raise a finger pointing at myself.

"Penelope," he repeats, "I'll remember that." He puts his hands into his pockets and the air is filled with silence again. "Well, uh, I gotta head out. But I'll definitely apply here and hope to hear back soon!"

I affirm, "You betcha."

As he's walking away, I'm turning to head back to the snack aisle.

I see him turning his head towards me from the corner of my eye. "Crunch is my favorite by the way."

I grin and giggle, "Oh, no way, mine too."

"I'll also remember that. See ya later!" He waves and winks.

Walking away into the distance.

I wave goodbye to him and go back to finishing up the snacks, unable to wipe the smile off my face, thinking that didn't go too bad.

In the following week, Alexander applies and is hired. We begin alternating between working the cash register, stocking snacks, and stocking up movies that are new in our inventory.

Jerry instantly loved him, because that meant he could have some "bro time" or "guy time" with Alexander during lunch breaks.

Jerry was now getting on my case about typical manager stuff. You know the kind of thing, like reminding me to clock in and out accordingly. Be nice to the merchandise and people (as if I'm ever mean, even when they drive me crazy sometimes). And the classic, "take a lunch break somewhere else!"

In case you were wondering, Alexander does get cuter the more you look at him! His eyes are so soft and his personality is astoundingly charming. He

makes me laugh a lot too! I realize we also have a lot in common. He likes movies
and cryptozoology like I do, although instead of romance he prefers horror movies
which I'm cool with. He recently moved here from Alabama as a way to start
over—don't know from what yet—and as I had correctly guessed, he is one year
older than me.

One rainy night when business was slow, we were hanging out near the
register, hoping for more customers to come in to make the time go by faster.

The rain droplets hit the window sill and dribble down as we watch the rain
fall, the sound filling the silence.

I looked at his name tag and notice it read *"Alexander C. Kirby"* instead of
just "Alexander."

"What's the C stand for?" I say pointing at his name tag.

He turns his head down to the name tag and quickly looks up "Oh,
Chupacabra!" He said jokingly and smoothly.

"Oh, shut up!" I laugh, "And my middle name is 'La Llorona,'" I say sar-
castically, rolling my eyes and laughing like an idiot.

"I mean, it definitely makes for good conversation."

"I suppose it does."

"Caleb," he admits. The sincerity behind his voice almost makes my heart
melt.

"Lorraine." Sheepishly, I feel my cheeks turn beet red.

Alexander laughs, "You have the middle name of an old lady, it suits you!"

"Well, when you're an old man, you'll appreciate an old lady like me!" I
stick out my tongue playfully and giggle more.

Stacks of paper slam against the counter, startling me. "Ah!"

"Woah, man!"

Jerry looks at us sternly. "Enough flirting, you two!"

Alexander and I look at each other, confused (we're both blushing a beet
red—is this what I think it is?) since Jerry usually isn't like this.

We guiltily look back at Jerry and he cracks a smile, eyes widening, showing his crow's feet and wrinkles. "Nah, I'm just messing with ya! God, you kids
need to lighten up!"

We both sigh in relief.

"Goodness Jerry, way to go and scare us!" I cross my arms looking at him,
pouting my lip.

"Awwww, Penny-pie, you know you love me! Now, how about I give you guys
an early summer treat and we close shop a bit early for the day?"

I uncross my arms. He knows how to gain my forgiveness, that's
for sure.

Alexander raises an eyebrow. "Really?"

"Yeah, why not? It's raining, it's pouring. No old man is snoring though."
He throws his hands in the air nonchalantly. "Well, I guess the old man snoring
will be me if I don't get my sleep apnea under control." He mutters to himself.

I'm ignoring that last part completely.

"All right, all right, Jerry! Thank you." I hug him and run to grab my bag.

Alexander follows behind me. "Wait up!"

The skies are grey and foggy. I pull out my umbrella and begin opening it
while I watch Alexander put on his raincoat.

"Let's walk home together, it's dangerous out here!" he calls out to me.

"Ready when you are." I call back.

We start walking together under the umbrella as he suddenly puts his hand over the handle, his pinky finger slightly touching mine. I blush and look away slightly. He blushes at my reaction.

He gazes over at me and his lips curl into a soft smirk. "I don't know how you walked home for a year in this weather!"

I look into his eyes. "I didn't want to bother anyone — or rather didn't have anyone to bother."

He looks at me, bewildered. "I'm surprised Jerry hasn't offered to give you a ride in this Florida weather."

"He has tried, multiple times, but I politely tell him I'll be fine."

He nods quietly, shaking his head understandingly.

I feel my insides start to warm up and I smile at him.

"Why don't you stay the night at my place?" he asks suddenly, "I could use the company. My parents are out on a business trip out in Georgia. Busy doing real estate finance stuff. It wouldn't hurt."

"Staying over?! Without their permission. I..I..It feels wrong to just barge in. I'm practically a stranger." Anxiety is the brain behind the operations and my mouth is on fire with how jittery I spit that out.

He smirks and lets out a laugh. "You're *not* a stranger to me. To them, yes. I'll text them. You'll be okay."

I take a deep breath and continue walking. "Okay."

He holds his fist out in the air. "Yes!" He exclaims.

"I'll let my mom know. Don't get too excited!"

"I'm excited to finally hang out outside of work, that's all." He had had an impish grin on his face as he kept walking.

I smile softly. "Me too."

We continue walking to his home in silence until we reach his apartment. It's a typical and ordinary brown building, four stories high with a huge parking lot in the front and a fancy indoor pool for its residents. Very convenient for the summer time.

We head up to the third floor hurriedly as I drag my feet across to wipe them on the outdoor rug carefully.

He opens the door and holds it for me, I quickly take off my shoes, placing them at the front door. He closes the door and hangs his raincoat to dry on a hanger.

We both sigh in unison.

"Want anything?" He perks up.

"Honestly, something warm would do the trick."

"I could make us some hot chocolate."

"Absolutely, that sounds great!" I beam at him like a little kid who just got their favorite toy.

"Take a seat anywhere, I won't be too long."

I wander around the living room and notice a photo of him sitting on top of a mini table and someone younger, but looks identical to him, with the cutest gap tooth I've ever seen. I look at it more closely and notice the freckles on his nose. The apartment was very artistic, with different paintings on the wall, an old retro television set. The couch is dark red with a soft feel to it, kind of like those old school couches you would see in those 80's shows. I sit down and feel a slight bounce.

"Two hot chocolates, coming right up!" He says as he carefully walks over with our drinks.

"Awesome," I gleam at him, taking the hot chocolate from his hand. I take a sip. Mmmm, this is homemade, nothing short of Swiss Miss.

He sits next to me and takes a few sips.

"I noticed the Polaroid of you with a little kid, is that your brother?" I say, breaking the silence.

His eyes soften. "Aw, yeah. That's my little brother, Callahan. He's fourteen. He is back home in Alabama in high school, doing his thing with our grandma until my parents get back."

"Aww, that's sweet! I bet he looks up to you."

"Definitely. I try to be a good role model for him. I miss him." He looks into his mug, deep in thought.

I place my hand gently on his shoulder. "You'll see him soon, don't worry!" I reassure him.

He gives me a soft smile. "Yeah, you're right. He loves the homemade hot chocolate mix our mom makes."

I let out a giggle. "Well, it *is* delicious!"

"Kudos to the chef!" said Alexander.

We finished our hot chocolate, getting lost in conversation. Talking to him felt like a breath of fresh air.

"Hey, I want to show you something" he says suddenly, getting up and putting our mugs on the coffee table.

"O-okay" I stutter, curious as to where this is going. For the record, I'm not just blindly following a guy I barely know. We're just coworkers? Friends? (Read: are coworkers your friends?) hanging out. Add to the equation the obvious slight crush I have on him.

He led me to his room, hand in mine. By the time I registered what was happening, we stood at his door. I looked down at our clasped hands, a deep blush spreading across my face.

He noticed, letting out a hearty laugh.

"You're so silly, just come in."

Inside, his room was definitely the opposite of his well-kept tidy living room. Posters of different things like "Frankenstein," "The Goonies," "Jaws," and there's even a poster of Brittney Spears. Interesting choice. I love an iconic queen. On the floor is an acoustic guitar with a neon black and green lightning strike rug. His bed sheets neatly tucked into his bed frame. Next to his bed was a window seat with two fluffy pillows and a soft wool blanket to lay on. I look at it with longing, thinking how nice it would be to close my eyes there for just a few minutes.

"Get comfortable! Mi casa es tu casa." he says, as I snap out of my thoughts.

"Ha,ha, okay" I take a seat over at the window sill and take a moment to look outside the window.

The rain was dripping down the window with a less brute force that we saw earlier, the dark clouds present, blurring the world outside.

I feel his body sit down next to me but I don't look towards his direction, just focusing on the rhythmic pattern of the drizzling rain.

"I always love sleeping when it is raining, it makes it so peaceful."

I looked at him as he said that, I felt the peace he described. "I love it too. I honestly feel at peace just sitting here."

"Well, I'm glad I could help."

I look down, biting my lip softly.

"Well, thank you for today! It honestly feels nice. I feel energized and social." I smile sincerely at him.

"You're always welcome here. Don't even have to knock!" he jokes.

I giggle. He looks at me with the softest brown eyes glistening at the perfect angle. "I wouldn't mind a cute girl like you keeping me company. Even at
work, it's just as fun!"

My eyes widen, a sudden warmth blooming across my cheeks. Did he just
call me cute?

Surely, I'm dreaming. Act natural! Act natural! What do I even do? After
moments of panic, I managed to say, "Thank you! It's been nice having someone
to talk to about these silly mythical creatures and my silly movies. My best friend,
Aimee, has been away at camp. You two would get along!"

"Oh, yeah? If she's just as awesome as you, I'm down to meet her. What's
she like?"

"Oh, she's funny, smart, super pretty, and protective! She also loves Beanie Babies."

"Beanie babies?! No way, my mom would collect those when she was
younger. She sounds great, by the way." He leans back, resting his back using his
arms.

"Definitely!"

The room was utterly still, the silence absolute.

"You know, I'm not really tired. Are you?"

"Oh, no, not really!" Truthfully, I was but I wanted to keep this conversation with Alexander going.

"Wanna play a game?"

"Sure, what is it?"

"21 questions!" He exclaims.

"Isn't that game reserved for middle schoolers addicted to their phones?" I
snicker and smirk.

"Uh, not exactly. I make it fun by being an adult playing it, not a middle
schooler." He sticks out his tongue sprightly.

I laugh and roll my eyes, "you're a dork!"

"A *funny* dork!" he corrects.

"We can make it fun, let's do it!" I say.

"Okay, you start. After all, ladies first." said Alexander.

"Hmmm… what's your favorite color?"

"Green. Yours?"

"Periwinkle! A mix of purple and blue." I smile brightly.

He taps his chin with a question to think of, "Favorite snack?"

"Caramel popcorn!" It's the perfect combination of sweet and salty.
"Yours?"

"Sour gummy worms!" he chuckles, like a little kid, making a silly fish
face.

"What did you want to be when you grow up?"

"Forensic psychologist" said Alexander. "You?"

"A veterinarian. I love animals." I proclaim.

"Ambitious woman. I like it!" He grins.

"Yours is actually very fascinating, you must've watched a lot of serial kill-
er documentaries." I joke.

"Only after midnight when everyone was asleep," he whispers, "Keep it a
secret though."

After several rounds of this game, which I normally find silly, I'm actually having fun and enjoying myself. Seeing Alexander like this just makes me want to stay in this moment forever.

"What's one thing you've always wanted to try, but are scared to do?"

I pause and think intensely before I answer, "Lucid dreaming."

He nods and shakes his head, "That's dope! That's actually an impressive answer."

"Well, I have layers," I smirk animatedly.

"So, why haven't you tried it?"

"I just don't know how…how I'd snap out of it, to be honest." I fiddle with my thumbs.

"And you haven't asked your best friend to help you?" He asked quizzically. "It sounds like quite the trip."

"Definitely, being in control of my own dream and all."

"*Dream*ception!" he said matter-of-factly.

"Ha, ha, yeah," I murmur, a soft smile planted on my lips.

"So, let's do it together. Tonight. I say we've gotten pretty comfortable with each other." He stands up eagerly and looks at me like a golden retriever.

I hesitate. I look up at him as he stares at me with those bright eyes, my hands starting to sweat. I'm scared because I've heard scary stuff happens. Like I wouldn't even know what to expect other than trauma and reaching into my subconscious. I bite the inside of my cheek.

"C'mon, c'mon! Consider it like a 'I crossed it off my bucket list' kind of thing" he said.

"Hmm..but what if something bad happens, I don't know how much I can take." I fiddle with my thumbs nervously.

"Then I'll be right there with you. You don't ever have to do anything alone. Annnnnd, I wouldn't force you either. I just believe that staying in the comfort zone needs to be challenged sometimes."

He could be a lawyer with the way he's making these valid points. I mean, I know I need to live life a bit and not get too much into my head about it. I'm just afraid that I'll find things about myself that I may have forgotten. But there's only one way to find out. Silence and anticipation fill the air rattling my fragile bones.

"Okay, let's do it then."

"Awesome! I'll grab some pillows and blankets."

He comes back with the blankets, handing me a soft fuzzy brown blanket and I look at it, admiring the softness and fluffy texture. "I really appreciate you doing this with me."

He sits down beside me and smiles softly "No problem, besides I'm always up for an adventure."

"Tell me about it." I lay down and let my body melt into his bed snuggling into the blanket.

"It'll make for a great story about our first date one day" he laughs, looking at me, laying down beside me, leaving a small gap between us, exhaling and lowering his shoulders.

"You're such a dork, you know that?" I roll my eyes and smile. "Thank me later."

I reach for his hand as I begin to feel sleepy and nervous, not knowing what to expect. He holds my hand affectionately and rubs his thumb over my hand gently,

"It'll be okay" he reassures me as we lay there.

"I believe you." As I drifted off to sleep, I felt myself gently lift from the bed in an almost ethereal state, until my feet settled onto the floor.

"One and done, okay?" I look over at Alexander.

"One and done."

*My eyes open as I feel my feet hit some dark old wooden floors.*
*Dark green velvet suede walls enveloped around me, their soft texture hinting at the secrets within as I look around. "Woah.." I mutter.*

*"You can say that again," said Alexander.*

*Walking down the hallway, I see vintage style paintings of all the cryptids I've heard theories on. The Yeti, Skunk Ape, and Old Hitler. The Skunk Ape portrait seemed like the Mona Lisa with the way I felt its eyes on were following me. I move in closer when suddenly it pulls me in, it's fur soft and textured with the putrid smell of sewer water!*

*"Penelope, you've done so much for others, but tell me, what have you done for yourself?"*

*I swallowed hard, my eyes widened. "What?"*
*The voice is feeling closer now, but I see no sign of any creature or Alexander.*
*"All that time invested in learning about the creatures people thought were imaginary... is the imaginary world one you wish to escape to?"*

*My eyes widened, stinging with tears, "I know my family and I have gone through a lot, but I was only trying to make things better! That's why I got a job in the first place."*

*The room starts spinning like a rollercoaster you can't jump off from. All I see in front of me is darkness and hear the eerie creaky floors as I slowly step back. "Sometimes, doing better lands you nowhere."*

*I look behind me to find a door with a distorted "Help Wanted! Inquire Within!" poster hanging by a single door at the end of the hallway. I lost sight of Alexander. Could he be in there? I look back at the vintage painting and again at the door. "I can't keep tormenting myself like this."*

*I run over to the door, grabbing a hold of the doorknob and frantically opening it.*

*Inside was the Film Galore, how it normally was. The snack cart filled with snacks and candies, movie rentals, and the door to Jerry's office was in the exact same spot. At least I thought it was, but I couldn't shake off that unsettling feeling that something felt off. Very off.*

*I slowly walk in, tip-toeing cautiously with every step. I see different customers walk past the counter, but their faces were not of a human, but rather hairy and monstrous.*

*"Looking for something?" The voice, a low rumble, seemed to vibrate the very ground beneath my feet. I pivoted, my breath catching in my throat as my gaze climbed, and climbed, to meet a hulking silhouette against the twilight. Shaggy, matted brown fur cloaked a frame that seemed to stretch endlessly upwards, shoulders hunched in a predatory curve. A wide, lipless grin split its face, revealing a jagged fence of teeth, each one a needle-sharp ivory shard. A chilling glint sparked in its eyes, a silent promise. Then, with a guttural snarl that echoed in the quiet, it lunged.*

*I scream and run towards the cash register, throwing movies on the floor. Its large feet leave deep footprints on the floor.*

*I hurried to the cash register, opening the large cabinet with a black key. This key...I remember it. I used it when Jerry would show me secret files and black and white films.*

*I felt the creature's labored breathing draw closer, shrinking into the cabinet and pulling the door shut just as its fingertips brushed the wood. Inside, I closed my eyes, catching my breath in the sudden silence.*

*I open my eyes slowly then open the cramped cabinet. I carefully get out of the cabinet and look around. I'm right back at the Film Galore, everything appears normal. Everything is in order. I creep around quietly and look around the cash register. No people around though.*

*"Penny-pie!" I know that voice.*

*I slowly turn around.*

*Jerry scrunches his face concerned, "You look like you've seen a ghost! Where ya' been hiding?"*

*"N-nowhere, just tired I guess" I shrug.*

*His face softens, his hand settling on my shoulder gently. "Well, how about you stand by the cash register and look pretty like you always do?" He says and walks off when I pipe up.*

*"Thanks, Jerry, but where is everyone?"*

*He turns back around, "Guess we're slow today, maybe the scare of the Skunk Ape got 'em!"*

*My eyes widen and I look back in a frenzy.*

*"You know I'm only kidding with ya'. I just..I just know how much you love that stuff. I tell you what, why don't you take the day off tomorrow, I still need you now" He welcomes me into a hug. We stayed in the warm embrace for several minutes, and I realize that he really does care for me.*

*"Sure, sure." I blink and cover my face, composing myself heading behind the cash register. I check to make sure that all the items are present: the cash is there, the cash register works, the "Help Wanted!" sign is still plastered outside, and the key is there. The cabinet looks completely normal. Suddenly, my brain goes back to that moment in that dream where I was running from the creature. At least I'm out of it.*

*The door opens and the door chime rattles, as I slowly look and it's none other than Alexander. "Where the hell have you been?" I thought to myself.*

*He comes up to the counter and I take my time to look at him. He definitely looks like Alexander, but isn't—this man has green eyes, but the same haircut as the Alexander I know.*

*"Hi!" said the imposter.*

*"Hi there." I say calmly, ready to confront whoever this is.*

*"I saw the sign that said 'Help Wanted!' outside and was just curious about working here."*

*"Well, what do you wanna know?"*

*He pulls in closer and says jokingly, "How delicious are the snacks?"*

*I hold back a laugh as I remember the first time I met Alexander. I was busy getting snacks when he inquired about working here.*

*"Depends what your favorite is — let me guess, Crunch?" I say cautiously.*

*Surprised, he says, "Yeah, good guess on the first try!"*

*You mean, second try?*

*Quietness greets us once more as we gaze at one another.*

*"Have we met before?" I muster up the courage to ask.*

*He stops to think and shrugs, "I'm not sure... Don't think so! It is nice to meet you though —" he gestures trying to find my name.*

*"Penelope" I say, skeptically. What is even happening right now? Who am I talking to?*

*"So, about the job application, Penelope…" he smiles at me.*

*"Oh! Right, right…Well, you just apply online and my boss Jerry should see it right away and hopefully invite you for an interview."*

*"Sweet! I'll do just that."*

*"I can let him know that we have someone interested to get you in as soon as possible, just let me know your name first." I look down momentarily to put some coins into the cash register.*

*"Alexander Kirby."*

*My heart sank as I looked up at him. This has got to be a joke.*

*But this isn't him. This can't be. It has to be someone else.*

*I try to reach back into my mind for all the applications we went through, his name was surely there, but there's no way he looked like this.*

*"Yeah. Um, can you give me one second?"*

*"Sure!"*

*I quickly text Jerry that I'll step out for a quick breath of fresh air. Then I ran out the door.*

I wake with a jolt. I scan the room and realize I'm in my bed, everything in place. My LED lights never moved. The posters on the wall remain unscathed.

I'm not at Alexander's apartment. We aren't lucid dreaming together.
I look down and notice that I'm still in my work uniform.

Was that all a dream? I don't understand. I frantically begin checking my phone and find texts from "Jerry McDonald" in my phone.

"Hey kiddo! You excited to meet your new co-worker tomorrow?" The text read.

"You betcha! This Alexander Kirby will be my partner in crime!" My reply.

"That's the spirit, kid. Listen...you know I care for you like a daughter, so heed my warning here. There's been some reported sightings of the chupacabra in my area."

"Jerry, come on, you know that stuff excites me. Cryptids are my friends."

"Penelope...it's been some weird stuff, rumors that they've been taking on a similar form of the humans they've come in contact with, you know...the chupacabras. Just be safe and careful. It's why I always asked to take you home, can't trust anyone. Remember, a friend to all is a friend to none. Love ya, Penny-pie."

I looked at the text. I always knew he was just looking out for me. Could this have been the warning he was talking about? I feel naive, like my memories of the last several weeks are foreign and unreliable. I wasn't suspicious of him joking about chupacabra being his middle name, probably because I was too blinded by my own feelings. He never gave me anything to be suspicious of...until now.

I search my memories in vain—does the real Alexander Kirby have green eyes or are they honey brown? I lay back on my bed and close my eyes. Is there a real Alexander Kirby?

You tell me, because I'm lost.

# About Our Authors

# <u>About Our Authors</u>

**Not all of the writers featured in this anthology wished to be included in this section. We didn't forgot them, we're just honoring their request for privacy.**


**Cara M. Bassett** is a Missouri-based reader, writer, and bookmark maker. When she isn't reading or writing, she likes to walk her dog or play tabletop games with her family and friends. She enjoys exploring themes of love and sonder in her writing and has been telling stories her whole life. She has won contests and scholarships for her writing in the past and has been published in the *Magic in Progress* literary magazine.

**Ivan Davis** is an author, idealist and, above all, a visionary. Ivan was born in 2005 to a middle-class Missouri family. His family struggled while he was growing up, faced with the perils of our modern age, from job replacement to drugs in the home. Ivan persevered and is now launching his creative endeavors to elevate man to another level, another form in our ever-march.

**Shawn Fairchild** is originally from Appalachia, Kentucky but moved to Honolulu, Hawaii to attend graduate school where he received a master's degree in comparative philosophy. His favorite genre of fiction is "weird writings" like those of Lovecraft, Algernon, and even Chambers. In his spare time, he enjoys rock climbing, reading, writing, and playing his favorite franchise games, Final Fantasy and Resident Evil.

**Erik F. Hill** was born and raised in Michigan. Since 2010 he has been based in Los Angeles, CA. He has worked in the film industry as a writer, actor, and technician. He describes his writing style as unpolished, unrefined, and unrelenting. His work is infused with themes from art, science fiction, film, paranormal, high strangeness and extraordinary life experiences.

**Kyle N. Kolber** is a writer based out of Connecticut, who specializes in writing all sorts of fiction. Since the age of 16, after publishing his first book, he hasn't stopped writing, loving every second of its process. In his free time, you can catch him listening to loud EDM music through his Bluetooth hearing aids, playing video games, playing Flag football, or reading.

**Jeremy Miller** is a native of the great state of Iowa who likes to spend free time doing indoor things where you don't sweat like reading, writing, and playing games - both board and roleplaying.

**Victoria Nemethvargo** is a girl from a town small enough to think Harrisburg, Pennsylvania was comparable in size to Los Angeles. Her love of writing started in school, turning in 500-word essays with 1,000 words instead. At 22, she is taking the jump from working behind a restaurant counter to being the force behind a powerful pen. For Victoria, the summer of 2025 was one of change; from marrying the man of her romance-novel dreams to taking risks she wouldn't have dared a year ago. She isn't sure what twists and turns the story of her life will take, but she knows that she will be writing it for herself.

**Ashleigh Norris** was raised on a farm in a small town in Alabama. She is a mother, cosmetologist, and an accomplished poet who loves everything related to fantasy.

**Samantha Oliver** is a speculative fiction writer based in the American South, where the storms are loud and the stories tend to linger. She is currently working on her debut fantasy novel, Warhound — a tale of gods, rebellion, and the kind of strength that doesn't come clean. She balances writing with a full-time job and raising two wild-hearted boys who remind her daily that magic is real if you know where to look. Her work leans toward the mythic and emotional, often circling themes of loyalty, survival, and what we're willing to become when we've lost too much.

**Lynda Vann** was born and raised in sunny South Florida. Her love for writing began at a young age. She feels writing is her native tongue at this point compared to speaking (especially with new people!) Aside from writing, she loves baking, playing video games, watching anime, and reading.

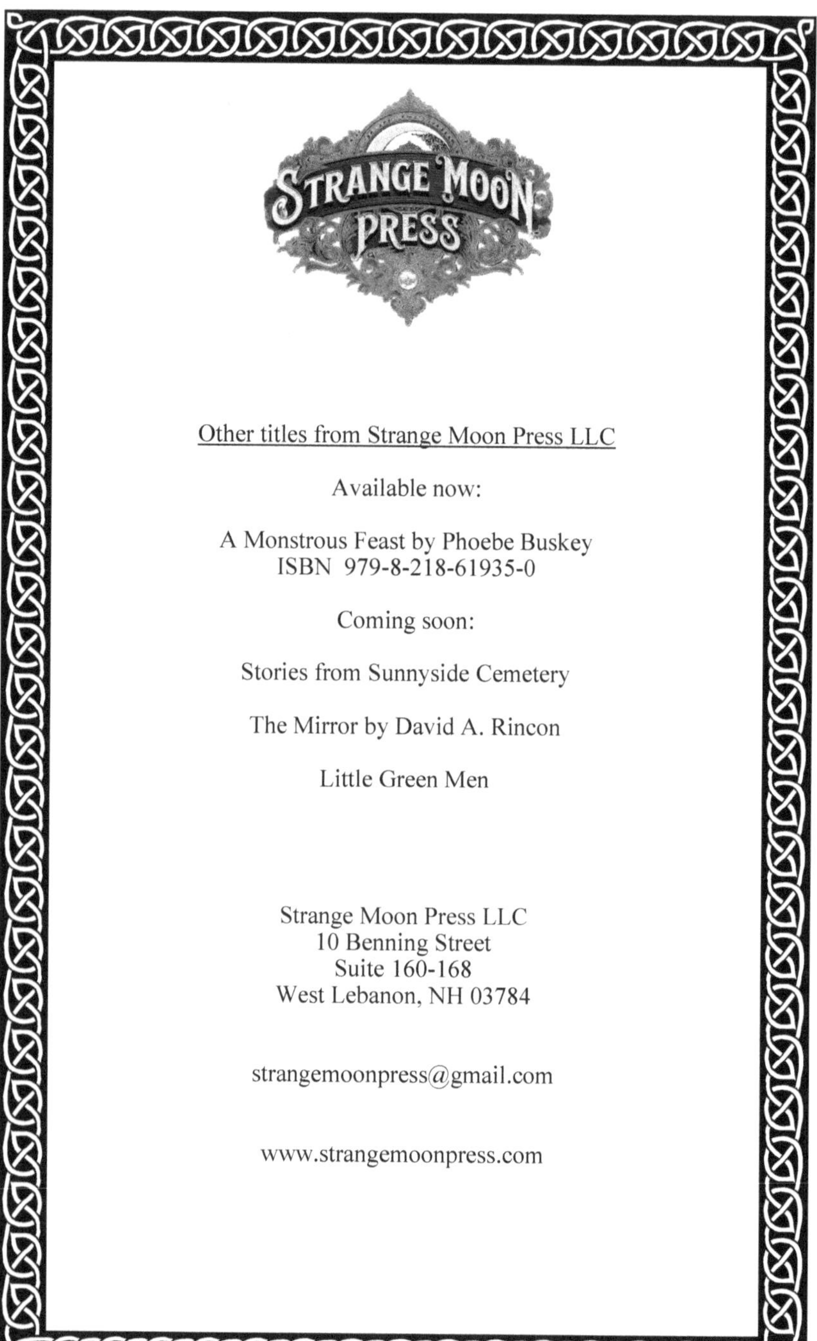

Other titles from Strange Moon Press LLC

Available now:

A Monstrous Feast by Phoebe Buskey
ISBN  979-8-218-61935-0

Coming soon:

Stories from Sunnyside Cemetery

The Mirror by David A. Rincon

Little Green Men

Strange Moon Press LLC
10 Benning Street
Suite 160-168
West Lebanon, NH 03784

strangemoonpress@gmail.com

www.strangemoonpress.com